Bittersweet

A Novel

Debra Geiman Colletti

ISBN: 978-0-578-66981-6
Library of Congress Control Number: 2020906242

For inquiries, contact debracolletti@gmail.com.

I dedicate this book to my earthly and heavenly fathers.

Acknowledgments

I would like to take the opportunity to thank a few people who made this book possible.

My husband, Michael, who tried his very best to stay quiet when I was writing. Thank you for loving me these past forty years. Thanks for being my "stone" and "my home."

My sons, Anthony and Nicholas, who have such good hearts. Thank you both for showing me the beauty of life through your eyes.

My mom, who taught me what unconditional love is. Thanks for always believing in me.

My sister and my brother, who remain my best friends.

My friends who are my family.

Josh, Air Traffic Controller, Shawn, Captain and First Officer, Nick, Aviation Pilot, and Michael, Air Traffic Controller. Each shared their knowledge and time to answer all my questions.

Carolina Forest Writer's Group, who pushed me, questioned me, and made me want to continue when I wanted to stop.

Jessica Tilles, my editor, who had patience and a sense of humor throughout this process. Thank you for taking away a lot of bodies in my writing.

⁸Then the voice I heard from heaven spoke to me again. It said, "Go and take the little book that is open. It is in the hand of the angel who is standing on the sea and on the land."

⁹ I went to the angel and asked him to give me the little book. He said, "Take it and eat it. It will taste like honey in your mouth. But after you have eaten it, it will make your stomach sour." 10 Then I took it from the angel's hand and ate it. It was sweet as honey in my mouth, but it made my stomach sour after I had eaten it.

— Revelation 10:8-10 New Life Version (NLV)

CHAPTER 1

"*Mayday! Mayday! Mayday!*" Jackson bellowed his urgent pleas into the transmitter he gripped in his palm. "We are Pilates PC 12, November 421 Zulu Bravo..." there was radio interference, "over the Atlantic Ocean at twenty-five thousand feet. Our coordinates are—" Static interrupted his communications. "We are suffering..."

The distress call received an instantaneous response from air traffic control. "What is the nature of your emergency? How many souls are aboard?" Silence hovered. "Are you holding an altitude of...?" Deafening stillness from the transmitter.

My mind replayed the events leading up to this moment. How was this possible? I was positive that pilot error was not the cause. Jackson was one of the most accomplished aviators in the state of New York. He had over twenty years of piloting experience. The logs he maintained were precise. My husband was meticulous while examining each craft before his arrivals and departures. Our son, Peter, who was a pilot in training, was nowhere near the cockpit when this trouble began. Therefore, I knew there could be no blame placed upon him.

Around ten o'clock this morning, with the sun shining upon us, we prepared for our mission trip. I overheard Jackson telling Peter and Isaiah, our other son, to start their appointed tasks. The heaviness of the bins prohibited Jackson from carrying aboard anything more than a few of the necessities. Although Jackson was a fitness fanatic like Peter, it was several years ago that his son far surpassed his strength and stamina. When his father admitted this to him, there ensued much light-hearted banter between the two. The family understood Peter needed to transport the heavier containers.

Jackson busied himself with paperwork. Peter walked close to his dad, hoisted one bin on his shoulder and flexed the muscles of his free arm. With a bounce in his step, he moved further away from Jackson. He then halted and spun around in a leisurely motion. Impressively, he raised the heavy container, pressing it high over his torso. Jackson grinned, shook his head and muttered, "Show off."

Peter beamed back at his father and rushed into the plane. Jackson called out to him, directing where to deposit the containers. Peter was meticulous as he unloaded each bin in the exact spot where Jackson instructed him. At a fast pace, he reappeared, running toward his dad. He taunted Jackson even further by seizing him around the abdomen and raising him off his feet.

"Whoa, Big Daddy, you appear to have gained several unneeded pounds in the last few months, while Isaiah and I have been losing weight these past two weeks. Have you been sneaking those sugary snacks while we are sleeping?" Peter poked him in the belly and settled him on the ground with a playful groan and dashed off, but not before Jackson could throw a good-natured jab to his arm.

In the corner, Isaiah stood, a smile spread across his delicate features as he listened to his older brother's provocation with their dad. At fourteen and a half, Isaiah's face still exhibited the charming features of a younger child. Maybe it was just my way of viewing him, clutching on to a son I never wished to grow up.

Isaiah's tone became serious as he reiterated several times, "Okay, you two, calm your jets down so I'm able to finish my duties!" Glancing over at his brother and father, he declared, "Geez, guys, someone has to be the responsible person in this family!" He turned away and moved to the side, viewing and counting the inventory in his head. Peter and Jackson had already carried several pieces into the plane, but there were other objects remaining in the hangar, still unaccounted for.

Isaiah's dad gave him the responsibility of managing the list of items so they would leave nothing behind. With immense pleasure, my youngest son enjoyed this task. Everyone agreed that any chore that removed him from performing physical toil was the right job for him.

The checklist was now complete.

Peter yelled, "Are we ready to hop on the jet of Captain Jackson? I ask you guys to note our seating arrangements. Isaiah, do I have to pick you up and place you on the airplane to show you, or do you recall the design after all the times we've flown?"

Isaiah rolled his eyes at Peter and added, "Go ahead, hotshot, remind us once again where you want each of us to sit! We've flown in the same pattern since it seems like forever, but you go on, tell me again, just in case *Dad* may have forgotten the positions of the seats!"

"Old man," Peter declared in a statement full of lightheartedness. "We demand you relax in the copilot's chair on this glorious trip." Peter directed his attention to me. "Mom, Madre, Mother... listen to me for once in your lifetime! You need to pay attention over here. Please open your ears to what I am about to tell you and my beautiful family."

I shook my head and continued chatting with Elise. With many flying hours achieved, she, too, had developed into a talented pilot. Jackson and Elise flew together on many outings. Both had a calm demeanor that proved invaluable on several recent trips.

Elise beamed at Peter.

"Praise you, Miss Elise, for giving me your undivided attention. I'm grateful that you appear to be the only one listening, but this information is top secret!" He bowed with a mischievous grin.

I was thankful Elise was also a good friend and knew the antics of my sons. I turned away from Peter to obscure the grin that might encourage him to keep right on speaking.

"It's okay, ignore me, Mom, but please don't beg me to repeat myself when you enter the plane and you are confused as to where you need to sit!"

"Lilly, hurry over here. Come on, you can do it! Oh, I know, Lilly, it's a well-known fact that you and Isaiah are not very good runners, but just try!" At Peter's tone, our plump golden retriever-mix wagged her tail and bounded over to him. "Lilly, let's pretend you are the mom since the *real* mother is not participating in our conversation." Peter glanced at our needy, confused dog. Still, she appeared excited with the extra attention she was receiving. She jumped up and her paws touched Peter's chest. "Off, Mom, off." He snickered.

Looking into Lilly's eyes, he continued, "Mom, you, are to sit in the seat located to the right of the craft, the seat diagonal to your dear companion. Not too far out of his reach if he tries to hold your hand. I recognize that stretching to touch you may be a bit of a challenge for your dear man to achieve since he's not in the best of shape. Although, we just never know what that partner of yours has the ability to do once he gets these romantic notions! I further perceive how troublesome it'll be for you not to sit in the seat right next to your spouse, but sorry, this is for the good of everybody. We cannot have your attractiveness disturb Dad flying the plane. Besides, now that I am the PIT of this craft, the seat will have to remain vacant unless I am in it!" He looked over at his brother. "Oh yeah, Isaiah, PIT stands for pilot-in-training, in case you forgot that, too!"

Isaiah mumbled something under his breath that Peter acknowledged. "Yes, I am well aware, little brother, that you, yourself, are in line to be the next PIT in the family. Just humor me, okay? As for you, since you are the last born, well, besides Lilly, you can rest in one of the back two seats. When Papa decides it's his turn to fly solo and take control of this plane, I know you will be so lonely without me by your side. I, the better-looking brother, will come to sit next to you to entertain you."

Isaiah's muttering grew to where Peter said, "Hush, I am attempting to show the logistics of my seating arrangements. After we refuel in Nassau, Bahamas, and we are halfway to Guyana, South America, our final destination, and the cabin crew distributes refreshments…"

Isaiah's face grew serious when he begged Peter, "You mean, Mom, right? She's the so-called flight attendant on this trip?"

Peter nodded in agreement.

"Phew, I'm relieved you didn't ask me to be the one to serve this time. Remember on the last trip we flew? I tripped and accidentally spilled your soda, and you pitched a fit! You were so furious I put a dark stain on your silly pink shirt." Isaiah's sincere look melted into a grin as he mentioned that pink shirt. "I did not care for that hue on you, to begin with!" He chuckled. "Seriously though, and I hate to admit this to you, but I am a bit confused. Why do we need Mom to serve a meal? We have been fasting for the past two weeks. I believe

6

we set a date to end the fast when we landed in Guyana. So, I can't understand why she would distribute any food. Besides, that—"

"Oh man," Peter interjected, "my people have no sense of humor. Yes, you're correct, no snacks, just water for you, me and Dad! Isaiah, please allow me to finish? I'll wake Mom up from her beauty sleep. She will honor you with her presence in the back. Around 6:00 p.m., Dad will request me to take control of this baby. It will be the old man's nap time by then. Hey, my peeps, why does it look as if everyone's eyes are bracing to pop out of their heads? I know I can solo pilot this sweet little plane. I mean, if *he* can do it, why can't I?"

Isaiah's big snicker caused Peter to erupt into a hearty roar of laughter.

"Brace yourself for a smooth journey, my tribe! That is, unless the "Man in the Sky" gives us a turbulent ride! Hey, Dad, isn't that one of your oldies but goodie songs?" Peter raised his voice and started singing. "The Man in the Sky keeps on turning."

Jackson peered up from his clipboard. "No, son, without a doubt in my sharp mind, it's: 'The Wheel in the Sky.' If you refer to my songs as ancient one more time, I will make sure you have more than a bumpy excursion."

Isaiah exploded with laughter. The noise of his musical tone was so contagious. Everyone in the hangar smiled at our family. These brothers provoked each other to see who could offer the best entertainment at mine or Jackson's expense.

I perceived it was my turn to be the brunt of one of their humorous remarks.

Wanting to outdo his brother, Isaiah, in his whimsical fashion, said, "Hey, Petey, we might be ready, but Mom is busy chatting and ignoring you, as usual! I'd bet you a million bucks she'd rather stay with Miss Elise than listening to your sorry attempt at singing."

Lilly barked at Isaiah's words. Lovingly, he patted her and expressed, "It's okay, we would never leave without her, although if she doesn't quit talking, it may force us to leave her behind."

My thoughts continued to whirl in varied directions. The weather broadcast on this cool spring day suggested nothing out of the ordinary that might attribute our aircraft to encounter this present trouble. My husband flew in appalling conditions in every state and country.

Jackson volunteered for Good Deeds for God, a charity that contacted him when they needed emergency rations flown into areas damaged by natural disasters. Whether a hurricane, tornado or floods, he jeopardized his life to carry supplies to the communities in the aftermath of these tragedies.

On every relevant occasion, I got a stabbing pain when a public announcement would broadcast on the television or radio of a recent calamity. His resolve had always been, "Yes."

Doing so forced Jackson to decline many family outings, and our special occasions rarely included him because he had his "other calling" to follow. I no longer interfered with what he desired to do.

In the beginning, it was troublesome to accept what his volunteer work involved, but I resolved to conceal the danger of his labor from our children. If I didn't monitor the television, when they saw the devastation, they became frightened they might never be with him again. It was painstaking for Jackson to try not to let their tears and anguish affect his decision. I recall both children hanging onto him and pleading with him not to leave them.

When they matured, they had a complete awareness of what their father's work entailed. Although we had fears surrounding his departures, we also were very proud of him. There was an unspoken understanding that these communities required him more than we did. We approved and even encouraged his absences that grew more plentiful over these last few years. So, once we admitted it was his calling, and what God sought him to carry out, he left the boys and me.

I tried to act brave in front of our sons. My anxiety rose, knowing the frequencies of natural disasters that transpired the prior year. Plenty of reports on global warming made me recognize that it would only become worse as the years passed. The more he flew, the greater the danger his trips evolved into. Jackson admitted that transporting aid to victims got tougher each trip. I questioned this because everything he did appeared so effortless. However, he described the governments in power grew more corrupt. They did not allow the rations to go where they were needed the most. On his recent assignment to Puerto Rico, he explained that truckloads of bins remained sealed; the stink of decaying food permeating the air, along with the smell of the rotting, stagnant water.

He told me most of the airplanes he piloted had reached their peak in mileage. Years ago, the funds overflowed in abundance. As of late, it was tough to solicit companies to aid this charity.

Over the past few trips, he had several narrow escapes because of the weather. Therefore, I made him promise to telephone me when he arrived at his final destination. The three of us stayed attached to my phone, willing it to play Jackson's chosen song of "Amazing Grace." Once the music from his cell phone vibrated in our home, we let out heavy sighs. Only after I recognized his deep voice on the other end did I smile through the tears cascading upon my face. Peter and Isaiah exhaled in unison and grinned.

On several trips, he found it troublesome to locate a functioning cell tower. Somehow, he always contacted us when he landed and spoke the same phrase. "I am protected again! Please do not worry. Pray for the people of this country who lost everything. Give my love to Peter and Isaiah. I miss you."

I had guilt because the communities he served were not a high priority to me. It's not that I did not care about the world, but if I lost Jackson, I would lose my world.

I understood the conditions he always flew in; I had confidence that today's weather would not be an issue. Not a cloud in the sky on departure from Teterboro, New Jersey, to Nassau, Bahamas, over five hours ago. On the last leg of our trip, when we were about an hour and a half from Guyana, there were clear skies. No forecast of any areas of disturbance on his flight plan.

Although my children had gone on several mission trips with Jackson, I never ventured with them before. I was looking forward to not only helping the women of this country, but excited about our well-planned vacation that would follow. It would be a perfect day for my first mission trip.

Perfect. A name many people used to describe my spouse. How often did I overhear that word associated with him? Every person encountered, every heart he inspired, proclaimed him to be perfect. Perfect father, husband, pastor... The list never ended, and everyone was correct.

I married Mr. Perfect, but what did he confess about this title they lavished upon him? He loathed it and dreaded the power the word enslaved over him. My husband told me when someone associated perfection with him, he suffered as if he might be sick. Once, he recounted to me how the bile rose into his mouth and he thought he'd have to spew the distaste from his soul. Jackson would frown when anyone suggested he was perfect, either sincerely or in a bantering manner. Several times I watched him turn his back on a friend who spoke that word so he would not embarrass them with the expression emerging from his heart.

Three nights ago, we lay awake in each other's arms. In the stillness of our bedroom, he clung to me and stroked my hair, telling me of the dread that surrounded him by having to hold such a grandiose title. His remarks, so serious and glum, suspended in midair. "Anna, when someone views another as perfect and when a crack appears, that is when others can truly find the value of the imperfect person God created. That is how God's grace shines from inside a person. I want others to know the real me. Perfection is a title only for God. If I remain flawless in their minds, I am their idol. I want them to know that my mistakes have made me a better human. Without the wrong decisions I've made, I would not be as intimate with God and desire Him as I do. I pray for everyone to see the true me and the flaws that are a part of who I am."

Although the temperature registered eighty degrees, and it was a hot, humid evening, an icy chill raced through my being, causing me to shiver at what he shared. Realizing, in silence, my cracks never turned me into a worthy person! Why would he want people to see the "real" him? Yet, I recognized the answer. He had nothing to hide; he never pretended to be anyone other than who he was. His sense of self never faltered.

Throughout all the times I loved him, he never lost sight of the person who God created him to be. This man held no pride. He accepted everything about himself: the good and the bad. Although no one ever found any wrong in him. This conviction, he passed on to his children. Jackson instilled in our boys how to love themselves the way God loved them. How I envied their confidences. It made me realize how much smaller I was when I acknowledged the unwavering trust they carried.

Now wasn't the time to ask how this could be happening. Jackson pointed the nose of the aircraft downward. Pitching the plane for the best glide speed. He did this to maintain momentum. My husband had no options on where to set the aircraft down. This would not be a safe landing. He understood and accepted it, but he would not agree that his family would not survive.

"Peter, get in your seat and take care of your brother. You can do nothing to prevent us from water ditching the plane."

Peter rose, clung onto the seats and made his way from the seat next to mine and went back to Isaiah and Lilly.

"I am not in control," Jackson prayed. "God, save my loved ones. I am ready to be with You, but don't let them die. Please, Father, spare Anna, and my boys. They have their entire lives before them; so much good they want to do. And Anna...You know what needs to happen, she—"

Before he finished his prayer, he turned and viewed the side of my face. He saw I sat silent and without emotion, staring ahead as if looking at nothing.

"Anna!" he yelled with intensity. "Prepare for a crash. What are you doing? I have rehearsed this before with you and the guys. I coached you on what to do in case of an emergency. This is it, Anna. There's no way you will survive unless you act now! You cannot sit there and pretend any longer. I cannot help you. You must put your life jacket on, at once! Do it immediately! Prepare yourself for a crash! If you are not interested in saving yourself, remember your children!"

His brutal and forceful tone stung my heart. I understood he used that firmness as a weapon to make me react, to shake me from the shock I was experiencing.

Confronted with the need to protect my sons, my reactions were always immediate and swift. Jackson understood this about me, but today, for some unknown reason, I sat staring ahead. None of this was comprehensible. It was as if everything he said appeared to be a mistake, and this was a nightmare. I imagined I would wake in his arms and touch the safety of him close by.

"Anna, are you listening? We are about to crash!"

His words echoed throughout the plane's cabin. The screams coming from Peter and Isaiah broke my trance. I now understood how dangerous it was. My seat was close enough to Jackson's to be able to view the tiny beads of sweat dripping into his eyes. His crisp, white shirt was drenched in the aftermath of his panic.

In all the seasons I had loved him, there was never fear in any of his expressions. Dread and anxiety belonged to me. Calm and disciplined was his demeanor. He kept it intact when everything in my world was falling apart. However, this was not the case any longer. I turned to Jackson; desperation filled his eyes. I was aware it required me to obey him.

With anguish, he tried to grab my hand, doing so not out of love, but out of necessity. As he released it, he insisted again we put on our vests.

I shook with violent trembles, but with sheer determination I put my life jacket on.

"Remember, Anna, how strong you are. Do not believe the lies any longer. You will continue without me. If I don't live, you'll survive. Those boys always needed you. You are vital to our family and the reason it is so amazing."

I stared at his moving lips. His gaze held me in a hypnotized-like state. Lies, lies…I tried to process this, but why? Why did he continue to torture me with those fabrications? By the look in my eyes, he comprehended I doubted every remark he made. He knew once again, nothing he said penetrated my heart. Yet, he too so wanted to believe.

He turned and shifted his attention to the boys who had reached well beyond the point of hysteria. "*Breathe!*" he gasped out above the noise. "You've got this. Good job getting on your life jackets. I have faith in you; you'll make it. I love you. You are our gifts from God. I'll miss you, but we will be together one day. Please take care of Mom. She'll need you more than ever."

"Dad, *no!*" Isaiah wailed above the unbearable cries of fear, suffocating the cabin. "What's happening? Are we going to die?" he cried out, his words mixed with fear and anger.

Before I realized what was occurring, I watched Isaiah remove his seat belt to move toward us.

Jackson shouted at Isaiah through his sobs. "You must stay seated, Isaiah!"

In a swift motion, Peter blocked his brother from moving toward his dad. He hung on to him so he had to stay in his position on the airplane. Peter's hands were shaking as he strapped his brother back in his assigned seat.

Trying to draw his dad's attention, Isaiah screamed at the top of his lungs, "I love you!"

Peter shouted the same, but it did not register if Jackson heard the emotions flowing from their mouths.

Jackson's response became hushed. I understood that hope in his eyes that conveyed, *I'll love you forever*, but not in this lifetime.

Then it happened: a calm, a peace, his anguish extinguished. His faith was deeper than any of our fears. God was answering his pleas; I didn't consider what else he had urged from God.

There were no words to express my emotions. I struggled to explain to him the secret things I bore in silence for so many years. I wished for him to realize none of this was his fault. I wanted him to see there was no way to fix my brokenness, regardless of how hard he or I wanted me to be whole. How ironic that his beloved Pilates was falling apart as my heart had. He could no longer hold me or the airplane together, even with all of his conviction in God.

Instead of pleading, I compelled myself to stare elsewhere with not a mention of what was stirring in my spirit. It was too late for any confessions, plus this had nothing to do with my past. I withdrew my eyes from him and concentrated on how to preserve my children. It wounded me to forsake him once again; however, I would not allow myself to dwell on this. I felt he could never accept what I attempted to do. He would forgive me, although it would be my final act of deceit. Jackson would not have wanted me to choose their lives over mine.

On a recent evening, our wonderful friends came over for dinner. Jean's husband, Robert, a teacher at the boys' high school, asked a baffling question. He mentioned that several weeks before, he quizzed his philosophy class. "Let's say there's a choice you had; which family member to save and why? I must tell you it amazed me at some answers my pupils provided." Robert stared at Jackson and continued to question everyone in the room. "What would you do?"

Jackson turned to me and, with urgency, responded, "No question, Anna over our sons."

What? I was at a complete loss on his answer. I did not allow this scenario to enter my mind. Why would I? Not a chance in hell I'd outlive my children! Much worse than that was how anyone—especially a father—would allow either of his sons to die? How dare he speak this out loud! Jackson planned for everything that needed to happen in his world, even in mine. In this entire conversation, he couldn't have been more wrong. I became distressed at his remarks.

I addressed Robert, in particular, and stated, "I hope that none of you think I am being rude by what I want to say. But, this conversation? There is no reason to discuss this, and it's inappropriate! I am sorry, but let's change the subject. Okay?"

Jean elbowed her husband hard in his overflowing belly. "See, I told you before we came, don't bring it up tonight! I am so tired of talking about this matter!"

Robert's chin hit his chest, and he acted as if he was a scolded little schoolboy.

Jackson responded by continuing to engage in this morbid topic. "No, Anna, we should examine this. I recognize you are uncomfortable, but this is something I need to discuss."

The silence in the house was overwhelming until Lilly's barking filled the void.

"She's got to go out." I glared at Jackson.

Jean, who appeared to sense the desperation in me, replied, "Come on, let's take her for a walk. Meanwhile, why don't *you boys* discuss how you both need to enroll in a course on sensitivity!"

Although things got lighter after we returned from walking Lilly, Jackson perceived my great unease the moment they announced their sweet farewells. I kept my distance from him and my iciness chilled the air. Jackson reached for my arm and urged me to sit for an explanation.

Since the so-called elephant in the room had invaded our house, he believed it was the right occasion to talk. How could I have known Jackson had a dreadful premonition of his death long before tonight? I learned of his forewarning once I became calm and sat across from him.

I listened to him revisiting the melancholy dream from a long time ago. It had lingered with him throughout most of our marriage. He interpreted it as a picture that never withdrew from his head.

I felt from the anguish in his eyes, he had been shielding me from the ghastly details. After he gave me a few of the specifics, I hushed him and advised straight out that I would not listen.

After that night, I did not grant him the right to express any of it further, either in my or the boys' presence. Besides, no way was this ever going to happen to our children. I recalled now what he spoke of, except for the ending because I would not let him complete the retelling of his premonition.

He understood, all those years ago, he would perish in a manner such as this. I wished I had supported him by allowing him to tell me about his dream. For years, he carried this monstrous burden, because I declined to let him release it. He might not have had to assume that sorrow alone if only I permitted him to speak of the premonition. Maybe this would not be happening and I could have changed what was occurring. Realizing the futility of that lament, I focused on how to shield my sons from their impending deaths. I had a responsibility as a mother. I always knew I was a fierce lioness, willing to lose her life to protect her cubs.

What mattered at this moment was my need to hold my sons, to shield them from death. But in that second, I knew I had no authority over theirs or my existence. Nothing or no one could stop this accident from proceeding. Even Jackson, who held such power over our lives, could not stop the plane from crashing into the sea.

I desperately needed to unbuckle my seat belt and express to each of them how we would survive this disaster. The mother in me desired to hold them close and soothe their cries. I hoped, when they had families of their own, we would tell stories of their heroics. We'd speak to their children about how brave their fathers were. Their families would realize how they displayed courage while facing death. Everyone would know they remained strong and never gave up hope. What a gift we'd share; a tragedy turned into a triumph!

Jackson's cry pierced above the clamor. "God loves you. I love you. Take care of each other. Be strong and do not fear."

With his arm hooked in Isaiah's, Peter reached for Lilly and pulled her into his chest to prepare for the wreck. Peter wept, his faint prayer asked God for absolution for the wrongs he committed in his heart.

Isaiah stared straight ahead, and I realized by his expression, shock detained him in his seat. There was no movement. He slipped into blindness on what was occurring around him. My soul told me what I recognized. I would not die without reaching them and expressing how much I loved them.

The plane, still gliding, seemingly appeared to almost touch the Atlantic Ocean. It was as if time had stopped and I was watching all this happen in slow motion. The oxygen was now scarce. I willed myself to stay alert, to focus on my boys.

My fear; the blanket, I had enveloped myself in my entire life, shed with a courage I did not know existed. I fought with every bit of strength I could muster. I tugged hard on my belt to release me from my burden. How was it possible there was no way to free me from a strap invented to save my life? Instead, it gripped me downward and prevented me from embracing them one last time.

Their helpless, blood-curdling screams, and loud growls from Lilly, filled the cabin.

"Oh, boys! Oh, Lilly!" I moaned. "Do not move. I'm trying to be with you. I'm coming."

It felt as if an invisible hand guided Jackson to lower his vessel as evenly as possible into the ocean. Still, the impact careening into the water battered my torso. It seemed as if every ounce of my being was stripped from my frame. The pain horrific, the agony shattering, my bones crushing into tiny bits of nothingness. I was in shock. Complete numbness replaced my suffering. Darkness filled my eyes. Blackness encircling. The shadow of death filled my head, and I was not conscious of where I was or what was transpiring. Silence hung in the plane's cabin; the pressure of descending and then the impact caused my ears to clog. I could not hear, but I saw the look of utter astonishment on Peter's and Isaiah's faces. Their mouths moved, and I was sure I could make out most of the words they were speaking.

"Dad," Peter yelled, "you did it, we are alive!"

Isaiah screamed nonstop. "I'm okay. Mom, are you hurt?"

Before I could tell them that I could not hear, Jackson scrambled to the back to seize the life raft. Unlocking the door latch, I stared as he jumped out of the airplane. Hurriedly, he yanked the cord to inflate the raft until it was afloat next to the plane. My husband used all his strength to tether the life raft onto our craft.

I clawed again at my seat belt. I ripped at my torso with no care of the damage I was inflicting upon it. I fought with my entire strength to remove myself from the seat. The buckle released, and I broke free to tread water. I wailed in the night's murkiness.

Jackson was once again on the plane. He yelled and mouthed words to me, but fear and terror overtook my mind. I was too distraught to remember what I should do next. I could see Jackson's mouth moving and the look of panic when I released the chord of my life jacket. The force of the pull catapulted me into the ceiling.

Through their hysteria, both sons tried to pull me back down. Neither could leverage their bodies to release me from the suction.

The air still silent, and although I could not hear him, I imagined my husband yelling, "Go, Peter, take your brother out. I'll get your mom!"

Peter pushed Isaiah hard to make him move toward the cargo door, while he held tight to Lilly. As both scrambled to exit the plane, I tried grabbing them and pleading with them not to leave me.

Both turned around, insisting on coming back to rescue me. Jackson yanked their arms to get them out of the plane.

After they jumped, I kept my eyes on Jackson. Although I could not hear him, he appeared to be yelling, "You won't die, God help me!" He looked crazed as he moved toward me.

"My boys, where are they? Are they safe?"

No sounds were audible. Whatever his answer, the silence of his words trailed off into the distance.

He turned aside from me as he struggled to get something out of his pant pocket. Jackson reached over and, with a swift motion, tried to deflate the jacket clinging tight around my neck. All I could see was the knife rising toward my face, and in a mode of panic, I used all my strength and shoved his arm away. With a look of shock registering on his face, I saw a huge gaping wound on his left arm.

"Oh my, God, what have I done? Oh, God, oh, God!" I yelled.

Jackson sliced my life jacket, deflating it, sinking me down into the water.

With his right arm, he guided me to the open door and pushed me out while following close behind me. Treading water, he gestured for me to swim east.

I turned toward where he was pointing and just as I did; he vanished out of my sight. "Where are you, Jackson?" I screamed. I tried to follow him back inside the plane, but the force of the waves pushed me further away.

Through the window, I saw him struggling to release the cargo in the rear. He was bleeding so viciously that I realized he would never make it back. Behind him, a fiery light silhouetted his profile. He reached out to me for the last time in his life.

"I'm sorry," I shouted desperately at him. "Forgive me. I killed you. Oh please, please, Jackson, please come back. I promise I'll get well. We are doomed without you! Your boys will die and it will be my fault. No one will locate us and my boys will pass."

Blackness, darkness, and then light. Light? Bright amongst the murkiness of the night. Not knowing where it came from, it appeared to be an invitation into an illumination. So brilliant, so serene; I desired to travel into it. Maybe my sons were alive in the lighted place.

Was this the white glow my best friend said encompassed her before the doctors declared her dead? I'll never forget her description of the encounter. She had surgery to remove a small cyst on her lung. It was not a serious surgery. The surgeons told her she would make a complete recovery and lead a long, healthy life, but something went amiss on the operating table. Her vitals crashed, and she was dead for five minutes.

There was no way Jackson could have known what transpired during the surgery. No one could explain why he rose and bowed toward the floor. The power of the Holy Spirit stirred, inducing him to sway back and forth. He continued to pray. My husband pleaded with God to spare the soul of this young wife and mother.

Mary informed me later that while she was traveling into the light, she floated above. She looked down at Jackson kneeling on the floor. He must have sensed her leaving the earth and going to Jesus. He prayed without ceasing; those pleas brought Mary away from the light. She wished to resist his cries because the glow was enrapturing and peaceful. However, Mary had this overwhelming awareness that the light would always be there waiting for her. Her heartbeat resumed and she returned to her body, shocking the surgeons and everyone in the room, except for my husband.

No! If this light is heaven, I'm not ready. I must save my boys; I am the only person who can. Those thoughts invaded my head as a violent rush of salt water penetrated my nose and lungs. A frantic surge of energy replaced the shock I'd experienced moments ago. I clutched onto an unoccupied seat, bobbing alone.

Out of the gloom, my husband emerged, floating toward me. Jackson's exquisite being was almost unrecognizable. I howled. There was nothing for me to do. The words came, but none emerged; the only sound was the carnal roar of a wife who saw death. Not death for the first time, but the death of a husband I adored. A man I worshiped.

There was no resemblance left of the partner I cherished for over twenty-five years. Somehow, Jackson's charred remains were almost beyond recognition. His blood was turning the cool blue waters into a mucky black hue. My gentle lover's cross remained around his blackened neck, glistening in the shimmering moonlight. I knew it was not Peter or Isaiah; they never wore their crosses.

As Peter often admonished Jackson and me, "Crosses are an outward symbol of religion. My faith is silent, Dad, I'm not boisterous like you!" Sometimes, Peter's language was combative. We understood Peter loved his dad and was trying to navigate the fine line of his faith versus his father's. It was rare that Peter needed to vocalize his beliefs to others. That's how strong his relationship was with God. Peter did not have to use words to share his devotion to Jesus. Everything in his life embodied the Lord.

As his lifeless body washed into the shadows, I shifted my gaze from this special man for one final moment. I would never hold or love this kind person again. His infectious laughter would never reverberate in our hearts. There would be no glimpses of the pure bliss he held for his family. He had gone home. Gone to a place he always desired.

My husband made one final choice in his short life: to sacrifice himself to preserve my life.

A multitude of times I overheard him tell our friends he was ready right now to be with his Heavenly Father. It was not something Jackson dwelled upon, although we all knew where he longed to be. If he brought this desire to light, his friends would twist it into a joke. They would tell him he needed to stay around to hold the church together and to keep us calm! After the laughter would die to a lull, everyone grew thoughtful. Mourning lingered in the air after these statements. We understood life would continue; it just would never be the same without his brilliance in our midst.

At this moment, there was no point to despair for his death. If I survived, I would grieve later.

"Goodbye, my love." I cried out to no one. The only noise that returned was in my heart. It was the empty echo of the crashing waves calling back and mocking the despair in my cries.

The horror of the crash became my forced reality. With Jackson gone, I had to live for them. I had to break free. Survival instincts kicked in.

Panic again overtook my common sense. I no longer had any sound judgment. Where were they? They had to be close. With the raft tethered to the plane, they had to be right here!

There was nothing to hear, and the darkness prevented me from seeing much further than a few inches in front of me. Wild, unmanageable thoughts made me think the raft had failed and so I plunged downward into the ocean, searching, never giving up hope. Were they trapped in the wreckage? Had their ears closed as mine had? I continued with my screams, believing that my cries would cut through the night. They were not dead because I declined to give in to any morbid thoughts. Somewhere in my mother's heart, I cherished the belief they were alive and I would find them. Though I ached all over, I willed myself to dive under the surge of the waves, resurfacing, gasping for air, gasping for life.

In the night's darkness, a sound popped inside my ears. Their voices of anguish filled the air. They were not below the water, but above it! The current must have carried them farther than I could imagine. The light! It was the emergency flashlight on the raft that Isaiah was using to signal in the deep, dark night.

Peter shouted, and high-pitched screaming came from Isaiah. "*Mom*, over here!" After their voices grew weaker, the steady and the hoarse barking of Lilly overtook the night.

Lilly, my ever-faithful companion, dove off the raft and into the murky waters to bring me to her brothers. My heart swelled, and I loved her more than I thought possible. I placed my bruised arm and shoulder on her thick neck. I linked my hand through her collar to help me swim forward. Lilly took me closer and closer to their voices. With a surge of strength, we swam back to them, to the two lives that were my only reason for continuing on. "Good, Lilly girl, good girl," I kept repeating so we would not lose our way or have the ocean separate us.

I feasted my eyes upon them, one after the other: my two handsome sons. I realized they were alive!

I grabbed at the side of the rubber raft.

The raft of hope, as Jackson had lovingly called it. It was an extravagant purchase. Jackson insisted the raft be larger than what the FAA rules designated. After the purchase, he left the receipt on the table on purpose. I remember opening my mouth, and, in an uncharacteristic tone, he admonished me and expressed his anger when he said, "Don't say a word, Anna. Can't you just trust me for a change?" I sulked in silence for weeks until I saw it was still in the garage and he had no intention of returning it.

The argument over the raft reemerged two months before this planned trip; in another exchange of heated words. In the past I usually won the few disagreements that occurred throughout the years in our marriage. Jackson would concede with a shrug and exclaim, "Mama knows best!" However, there was no winning this battle.

On this matter, he was inflexible. He refused to give in to my pleas. Still, I begged. I refused to contemplate how adamant he was. Jackson could not convince me this raft was more important than distributing new clothing to the ladies in Guyana! I insisted this larger raft was too costly for our family. I presented what I thought was a good argument and showed him how much money we could save if he traded it in for a smaller one. I called department stores to get prices on the gifts and clothing that I wanted to hand out to the outcasts. These women and children were the reason I was on our mission trip. He knew how much this meant to me. However, from his dream, Jackson realized he would, someday, need this vessel to spare lives. He told me I must listen to him. God told him to make sure we had room aboard for it.

Jackson often recognized God's instructions. When he did, he submitted to His authority and rarely questioned His voice. Jackson never disobeyed God. After lecturing me about this, I recognized it was not worth arguing any longer. Everyone who understood my husband knew he put God first in his heart and allowed Him to lead him on His path.

As I touched the raft, I had the overwhelming knowledge that it was the last of Jackson's two final offerings. Jackson tried to save his family without considering himself. Did he realize what he was doing? For now, though, none of that mattered. What was important was the God who filled our home and guided their hearts had spared our lives. I felt relieved.

Now is the time to thank Him as I had not done in years. However, the voices of darkness overtook my thoughts. I demanded to ostracize them before they robbed me of one more minute of my existence. One more minute that turned into many more years.

CHAPTER 2

When was the last occasion I talked to God? Yesterday? Last month? A decade ago? At every meal, I would bow my head and repeat, "Amen." I served lunches to the homeless every Thursday. I wed a minister of a Christian church! How could I not recollect when I last communicated or sat in His presence, or even recall my relationship with God? What was I moving toward or, perhaps, away from in all those seasons?

I forced my mind to travel back, replaying in gradual motion and retracing the memories in my life. With an unforeseen and sharp blow to the abdomen, I recalled. Horror and doom came flowing out and spilling over into my core. Without warning, the ominous event was rising in my head once again.

At a seminar I attended years ago, a psychotherapist trained in traumatic events, explained how a smell or a sound could create a ghastly incident to reemerge. Anything could trigger that trauma. It could happen in an instant, or at other times a person could suppress it for a lifetime.

For me, it was in my past, or, perhaps, it was another life ago. I was twenty-one, and it was the last time I communicated with Him, a moment that forever altered my life.

I thought of Karen. Her forgotten pain was different. Yet, in ways, it was like mine. She was a fine, yet lonely lady from our parish, who was courteous and cordial. She volunteered on Sundays with the babies during the service. Although she smiled often, there was an air of grief about her. It was as if she bore a secret and granted no one access into her world.

On a gloomy and stormy Sunday during communion, after they laid the bread in her hand, the dark memories engulfed her mind. The sniff of that bread unleashed the evil of the neglect and deprivation she suffered as a toddler.

Her explosion of pain appeared right on the altar. Again, my spouse moved to the rescue of one of his members. He escorted Karen out of the sanctuary. In the car, he spoke to her while she sobbed. I rushed out with them, hoping I might soothe her. Karen asked Jackson if we could be alone. My caring husband searched my face, and I nodded permission for him to leave. I recognized the intensity of the anguish she was reliving, yet I did not understand how to relieve the pain pouring out from this young lady. My instincts told me not to say a word, just to listen. Doubled over in severe pain, she held her hands on her womb. Sobbing and moaning as if to ease the suffering, Karen's deep brown eyes filled with an infinite volume of tears.

Rocking back and forth, as if this, too, would release her burden. She sat upright and gripped my hands and announced, "I recall now. I need to explain what happened. I believe you might understand my grief."

Dread invaded my thoughts. Was it conceivable that someone had learned of my secrets? Not even my husband understood the depths of my sins. I tried to refocus my mind off of myself and to remain strong and supportive, not daring to think again of my black dread. I listened while she recounted the years of abuse.

"My father's excessive drinking allowed him to close his heart to me. During the day, he wept and declared that he would never punish me again. Late at night, his demons stole any of the good inside of him. He continuously denied both food and love. It progressed this way for years until he slipped and shattered his back and could not care for himself. My mama allowed my grandma and grandpa to raise me from the age of seven until I left for college. I did not report the abuse to any adult because I was too afraid to tell my grandparents how much I suffered. The only clue they had was the night terrors that filled their home every evening. When they probed me for answers, in their loving ways, I lied and told them I just missed my mommy and daddy. My mother finally admitted to my grandparents that my father was an alcoholic. She did not elaborate on the extent of the abuse, only saying he was angry on different occasions. My grandparents never spoke to me or anyone about this because they thought this was the way to protect me from the misery. As years passed, I allowed the memories to fade, but deep in my conscience, I invariably assumed there was something wrong with me. I thought I was a damaged, broken woman. I trusted no one, never understanding why. But because of everything I've remembered, it's like I'm looking at myself from a distance. It will be okay. I finally understand none of this was my fault. I was merely a young child and did nothing to deserve the abuse from my parents."

I cried for her and every lost human who had a life that bore so many dark secrets. It was inconceivable to me how one could continue for years in life with pain buried deep inside their hearts. Even if those terrors remain suppressed for your entire existence, they still grow into a silent part of who we assume we are. It repulsed me to learn about the revolting acts this child endured.

Not one individual in the congregation had any knowledge of the horrors of her past. I caressed her sweet face in my hands and let her feel my deep, tender feelings for her.

Her face emitted a soft glow, she said, "I will be all right." With that, she touched my hand. "But you, what trauma are you burying?"

My anguish consumed the space in the car. There was no holding back and a reservoir of tears unleashed. I tried to express to her how it mortified me to think of my past. She was the one who had uncovered horrific details that she had bundled up all those years. Karen was the one who required sympathy, not me.

As if glancing into my soul, she whispered, "I do not know of your former life. Only that you do not have to carry your secrets. I have looked into the misery in your eyes since the day we met. You need to understand—you, too, are loved."

I knew now she had no knowledge of the mystery that consumed my life. She did, however, have a sense of the hopelessness that filled my days. I melted into her arms and we held each other until the tears were long gone. We continued to meet in secret for months. I never divulged the origin of my damage to her, but she tried desperately to help me release the heavy load I carried alone.

Once she revealed to the public the terror and barbarism of her parents' acts, she had the power to hold those who tortured her accountable. With Jackson's encouragement, she began her journey of forgiveness. She absolved her father (the abuser) and her mother (the silent abuser) for the actions of horror they caused upon her tiny being. Forgiving them restored her. Karen used her past to start a support group for women who suffered at the grips of another. Her parents even became members of our church. They acknowledged the depths of the evil they inflicted upon their daughter.

Their family grew into an influential force in battling the darkness and secrecy of child abuse. Jackson proclaimed they broke *the chains of the fathers* because they accepted responsibility and repented for their past.

It took a long time for me to understand how the submerged memories invaded her on the day of communion. Until now, I never accepted what had taken place in my former days. When the darkness reemerged, I thrust it below into my being. I was secure by doing this. Now, it was too late.

The slow and steady motion of the sea now unleashed the forbidden memory of my past life, pouring down a storm of dark dread. I had no breath. Everything closed in around me. With a renewed sense of defeat, I tried to force the voices out of my mind. I frantically clawed at the surrounding air. The swell of evil invaded my breathing. This desperation clung to me as I tumbled onto the raft, fighting back the tears and struggling to speak to my boys. I craved not to dwell upon my panic, to will my mind to concentrate only on them. I had to force myself to remain in the present. If I let these memories in now, they will remain with me for eternity.

Often, I disciplined myself to press them deep into my core. If I allowed those voices to admonish me of my past, I might not stay alive or even desire to live. My mind swirled, the voices taunted and reminded me of my iniquities. I shook my head to eliminate the murmuring coming from within me.

Never could I return to the person I was, and once again, I died another death. My mind hungered to shut out all the accusations that now lay open in my heart. With Jackson gone forever, I recognized there was no way to ignore the darkness of my soul.

As the sinister black clouds swept across the night, a full moon appeared above our heads. I welcomed the dim light to aid my vision.

I shifted my gaze from the dark to my children. I allowed my heart to turn from pain to my only source of joy. They were unhurt. We survived the crash and we were together!

I did not have to lift my shirt to know deep bruises covered my abdomen. I probed both my sons to determine there were no fractured bones or injuries that called for immediate attention.

Peter's crisp, laundered blue polo shirt and khakis were torn in several places. The boat shoes he had just purchased remained secure on his feet. His eyes expressed shock, although out of the three of us, he looked to be in the best physical condition. Though forlorn, he tried to remain stoic for me, until I sobbed, my tears becoming uncontrollable. Peter's body language gave away the braveness he was trying so hard to portray. My son fell into my arms and held me so tight, forcing me to move away from his longings.

I turned my attention to poor Isaiah, trying to stand before me, yet appearing so insignificant, as if he had shrunken from the wreck. He was trembling with such intensity it caused the entire raft to shake. I embraced him and continued whispering, "It's okay. We are alive." His shirt was hanging from his shoulders and torn around his stomach. I could see the ugly marks and discoloration forming on his torso. The jeans he wore had several gaps in the fabric, and his loafers were no longer on his feet. He must have taken them off during the flight and in panic never put them back on. I studied his uncovered head. I could not remember the last time I saw him without his hat, other than in church that is. His ever-present Yankees hat, long gone.

This was the hat Jackson purchased for him at a baseball game. Peter always rooted for the Red Sox and Isaiah for the Yankees. We attended at least two games a year; every time it was a very long trip home. The chiding began the minute we left the stadium parking lot and finished, in the same manner. We endured silent rides home from one whose team lost, but much chitter-chatter from the other brother whose team won. Jackson thought this banter was funny. I found it annoying because it proceeded until one lost their temper halfway home. Jackson, once again, had to assume the role of a serious referee. Our sons never caught on how he secretly thought the entire segment of arguing was comical. They'd never outgrow this childish competition of whose team was the stronger one that year.

Although I preferred not to be at these games, I grasped how much this day meant to my family. So, I braved the heat and hysteria to be a part of this happy memory they cherished. Jackson often teased me how out of place I looked. He never ceased thanking me for stepping out of my comfort zone. I rolled my eyes and told him, "You owe me big time for this!" Jackson treasured that I agreed to go with them. He had a charming thank-you card hiding somewhere for me to open. It never ceased to amaze me how he wished for my happiness.

In private, I smiled to myself, reflecting on how my "boys" and the "big boy" had the finest moments of their lives. Even if I disliked the games, I enjoyed seeing the look of pure joy on each of their faces.

He only accepted the lake house vacation and these tickets because the congregation insisted. Even after they were in his hand, he had guilt for taking these gifts. It wasn't until he looked at the bliss on the boy's faces that he confessed it was okay to receive these contributions and to have gratitude for them.

Most years, he held the church picnic the weekend after, so he could personally thank each member. He made it a point to show the parishioners the pictures of our grins, although we giggled at my fake one! They loved hearing the stories of our time at the ballpark. These people recognized he needed time with his family. They made it a priority to take up this collection, to display their admiration for their spiritual leader every year.

With those pleasing thoughts of Jackson and his leadership, my heart skipped a beat. I now peered at dear Lilly. From what I could tell, she had sustained no injuries. Our dog obediently settled in the raft and I quickly examined her vast body. Her thick, curly coat of fur made it difficult to determine if something was wrong. Lilly stared at me with such trust in her eyes. I realized even after all we endured, she still had confidence in her family. Her heavy panting had me feeling uneasy, but I thought it must be from the stress of the crash.

Their sharp voices broke the silence. Frantically they called out, "*Dad*, we are over here." I longed to cover my ears from the sound of my sons' cries overtaking my heart. Lilly's hoarse barking continued right alongside their pleas. It was as if she also sensed the need to recover her master. I turned to them. I observed in their faces and discovered in their voices the hope they carried.

"*Dad! Dad!*" Their cries pierced my thoughts. Their pleas became more demanding.

"We are over here! Mom's here! We need you!" Peter cried into the night.

Isaiah dangerously rocked the raft by flinging his arms left and right, hoping the motion might attract his father. There was an increasing sense of hopelessness in me with their desperate pleas and frantic gestures.

"What's that? Shine the light over there," Peter yelled to his brother. "No, the flashlight, don't set off another flare. I told you not to do the first one. I knew Mom and Dad would find us. Now we only have one left!"

Isaiah had set off a flare too soon, I thought. That must have been the fiery light I saw behind Jackson. Oh my God, that's what burned his body! I would never tell them what happened to their father. I would only let them know it was my fault he died. Isaiah would never forgive himself for this mistake.

Peering into the dark sea, I tried to determine if what I saw was their father's body. If it was him, I must shield them from this image that they would never get out of their hearts.

Peter glanced further down and yelled, "It's only a piece of the wreckage."

I cannot go through with this, I thought. *I do not have his courage.* He had the knowledge to keep us alive, and was the strong one. His hands were steady when mine shook. When I was breaking apart, he was busy putting me back together. I required his directives to tell me what to do. What to say. How to act. There was nothing in me capable of carrying my boys to safety without him.

They were the most protected when they were with Jackson. He always led them with Godly counsel and wisdom. They revered him. They never had enough time together. Most kids their ages were out with friends and had girlfriends. Not Peter and Isaiah. Their favorite part of the week was our Friday night ordering pizza and playing board games.

Two weeks ago, after dinner was over and we put everything away, they listened to the tales of Jackson's recent mission's trip. They loved the stories regarding people he touched throughout the world. They sat in awe as he relived every detail of the trip. His tales of journeys throughout the world enthralled them. Their eyes lit up as if they, too, were in a foreign land spreading the gospel of Jesus.

At one point, he got up from his favorite chair in the family room. His voice filled with raw emotion. It betrayed the struggle that was regularly going on between his head and his heart. It was hard for him to accept we had an abundance of blessings, while the children from outside the orphanage had nothing but dirt to eat. He talked about the kids at the churches and how they danced and sang with happiness when they saw the meager supplies he offered. They surrounded Jackson and held on to him lovingly. These children had no worldly objects in their lives, but expressed pure joy through their movements with the music. Their innocent melodies uplifted him. He described it as feeling he was in paradise.

After passing out the supplies and there was nothing left, these children continued to hold his hand. He'd look around at our faces and raise his hands up in the air. My hands are empty, but still, they hold on. They realized there's nothing left, but they won't let go.

The people of this country were not full of the materialistic things of this world. No, they overflowed with the love of Jesus. At a young age, they learned who their Savior was. They grew into such fine young followers, and several even became leaders of their own people.

In the gravest parts of Jackson's talks, he told them of a group of Muslim villagers that did not allow their children to hear the gospel or receive a gift from our church. Isaiah turned his head away from us. He covered his face so his tears were not visible. He reached for my hand. His heart ached for the lost. How special he was, so sensitive and loving.

It was then that Isaiah mentioned when he became a junior in high school, he had a plan to apply to seminary schools. He claimed there was a calling in his heart since he was a young child to start a church in Uganda. Jackson had always wanted him to do mission work. He believed that would be Isaiah's vocation. It was a subject that Jackson only discussed with me. Their father desired the voice of God to lead our children, not the dreams of himself. He was ecstatic with this news; his son will change the world.

Since his birth to the present time, they labeled Isaiah a strong-willed child. It was very challenging to raise an adolescent/young man that was so determined. We tried to believe this trait would serve him well in his life. When he was younger, there were frequent nights I questioned my attempts at parenting him. We often declared he came out of the womb screaming, "*No!*" Although we joked about this later in his life, there wasn't much humor in the way I handled his determined mind. I can still hear his voice arguing back when I casually mentioned in conversation the skies were blue.

"Hmmmmm," he maintained, "no, they are gray..." and on and on, the argument continued.

It ended with me yelling, "I do not wish to debate this!"

Although he had such a mindful spirit, the most important part of his being was that his heart and Peter's were kind and pure. Both were born to be leaders. Isaiah's passion was to save the unbelievers. I was proud that he cared more deeply for others and was less concerned for himself. This quality would assist him in being a good leader of a church. He was so much like his father, knowing his purpose in life.

Oh, how they loved and honored their dad. They were so much alike in their love for Jackson. The strange part was, as strong as their love was for him, they loved me for different reasons.

Peter once had to write a paper for his philosophy class. He withdrew into his room every night after dinner. Other than going to school or to eat, we never saw him leave his bedroom. The question was: if you had to choose someone to save, who would you choose and why?

The minute I heard the topic, I was positive he'd pick his father. I was okay with that because I understood their unshakable bond. I never entertained any thoughts it should be any different from the way it was. I wanted them to be like their father and not like me. I held onto no envy of their relationship. The three of them belonged together; I was more of an outsider in this family. It was not something that we spoke out loud; it was this knowledge I had since they were young children.

However, that day when Peter got home and told me to read his paper, I cried for days. He did not choose his father as I had thought. He picked me. It took months for me to get the courage to ask him why. His words still echo in my heart to this day.

He explained that his dad was strong, that he had a life filled with God. "You, Mom…you are the fragile one. You need protection because you're like a bird that had a broken wing. A bird that could never fly." This image haunted my mind because this was me. I never realized my sons saw it, too.

I was a wounded soul, although others perceived me in a different light. They saw me as an outstanding person who upheld all the responsibilities that came with being married to a pastor. They often spoke about my own sacrifices right alongside my husband's. Everyone told me they could not manage what I did every day. I would look into their eyes and think, *Why are they saying these things?* They stated how hard it must be that he repeatedly got the glory while I stood on the sidelines. These same people commented on how I gave up on a lot of opportunities while my husband was away helping others. What none of them realized was all Jackson denied for himself to keep me from leaving this life.

For my boys, I also went above and beyond for them. I left my career as an RN at the largest hospital in our town to be home with them every day. As small children, I did not allow them to get off the bus without my being at the bus stop. I drove them to all their sports practices. I was the homeroom mom from kindergarten to sixth grade. When they no longer needed me at the school, I made sure I was on the PTA.

I was constantly there for them. Physically, that is. I wanted to please my family and for everyone to think I was a good wife and mother, that we belonged together. I needed people to see me the way I saw my family. Our community believed in me this way. My perception of myself was like I was looking into a mirror with no reflection. No matter how many accolades I got, I accepted nothing of what they said about me.

Still, I tried to be the best mom and the best wife because that was what I knew people expected. I could disappoint no one. I had to prove I was *good*. I was a good mother and a good wife. I was really *good* at acting this way, that is.

While everyone was fast asleep with no notice, the pretense would sometimes shatter. When our home was quiet, and the moon and stars illuminated our bedroom, the real me emerged. I kept her a secret for many years. I could never grasp who this person was. Was I evil? Were they lies I believed all those years that turned into truth? I only allowed these unwanted accusations to submerge in the darkness. It was not every night my heart and mind were full of unrest. In the morning, it was a very rare thing I even dwelled upon the war that dissected my soul.

Jackson knew of this division from some of his parishioners who experienced this wrestling within their spirits. He witnessed this raw emotion with several of his parishioners over the past few years. My husband knew what to do when someone was suffering from PTSD. They trained him on how to react in a situation such as this. Jackson had taken several counseling classes. We had many veterans in our church. He was well versed in the trauma of those who fought for our country in the Middle East.

When they came to him in private for help, he had a gentle gift of guiding their thoughts and emotions. Despite their shock and wounds lingering from the devastation they had seen daily for years, my husband brought the veterans through some of the roughest periods in their lives.

I will never forget the first time I personally viewed this torment of another's soul.

It was an ordinary service until Captain Edwards leaped to the floor. He shouted, "Get on the ground! We are under attack!" A child had accidentally dropped his Bible on the old wooden floors of the church.

Jackson stepped down from the pulpit. He lay on the floor, covering the honored veteran. The people sat helplessly

46

watching as the captain convulsed in sobs of fear, anger, and grief. Jackson did not leave this man's side until he was at the hospital for yet another time in his young life. My husband held his hand, even while the medicine dripped in this warrior's blood through an IV. Jackson never once let go until the soldier drifted off into a deep and dreamless slumber.

How Jackson's heart ripped in two after this episode. This event had hit close to home. It opened up wounds that Jackson thought had healed.

As a young child, when his father took him to air shows, he told everyone someday he'd fly a plane. I still have the pictures his father took of the airplane swooping over his head. He held a look of sheer joy, and his dad mentioned it was what he was born to do. As he grew older and developed into a man, he wanted to be a pilot serving with our troops overseas. To defend our country was something Jackson had dreamed of doing. He graduated at the top of his class in flight school. On the day he left to sign up for the Air Force, one could only imagine my shock when he arrived home. He told me God had something else in mind for his future. I nearly jumped out of my skin.

My husband explained to me that right before he put his signature on the paper, he heard the voice of God. This blindsided me. Selfishly, I was angry he changed career paths without my knowledge. Although deep down, it relieved me he chose not to go to war.

God revealed to my husband that he was to serve Him in ministry. Even before Jackson became a pastor, he had listened to God and was obedient to His callings. Because of his respect for God, Jackson gave up all his hopes and desires to save lives overseas. Little did he know that he would someday fight for the souls of the people in our country, mine included.

Shortly after the episode with Captain Edwards, for the first time I can remember, he voiced questioning God. Not understanding his decision on why he did not go overseas as he constantly thought he should. Why did he become a pastor and not a fighter? He kept repeating how ashamed he was. Others fought and lost their lives while he was still here, alive and well. No matter how much I reminded him of God's calling on his life, he grew into deeper despair. He began withdrawing into himself and shutting out all our concerns. He was becoming a man no one recognized. Even the boys tried to get him to laugh and talk. He would take many long walks alone at night. It was a terrifying time to witness this man of passion become almost passionless. Jackson admitted he no longer believed he should continue in his pastoral duties. There was no doubt in anyone's mind that he needed to get counseling.

As a family, we approached him to seek help. Our first conversation was a disaster. Jackson's anger rose from a place that did not belong to him. He argued that he would not go to a professional for guidance. He insisted God would heal him. He became frantic, thinking the people at church thought his faith wasn't strong enough. Jackson was fearful and embarrassed to confess he needed help. He worried the council would think he could not run a church any longer.

This was the furthest thing from the truth. Our church was consistently supportive of Jackson. They knew he now needed their help. For all the years he had unselfishly put them first, they wanted nothing more than to do the same for him. We all felt powerless for this remarkable man who was crumbling before our eyes.

One evening, Captain Edwards came over to visit. Whatever he told my husband in his study, it did not matter; he finally accepted he needed professional help. After he left, I saw light returning into my husband's eyes and I knew he would be well again.

That next Sunday, Jackson announced to the church of his need to take time off and receive care from a specialist in town.

Jackson spoke out loud what he silenced for so many months. His voice betrayed him, causing him to give way to all his doubts. He slumped down on the pulpit. With a voice filled with raw emotion, he admitted he had become overwhelmed by the darkness.

His voice quivered with pain and uneasiness as he told the story of when he was a very young child, and a specialist diagnosed him with severe depression. I held my breath when he began speaking.

Although I knew Jackson had melancholy as a young boy, I never realized the severity. How strange he kept this secret from me after all these years. While he was talking, he kept his gaze on me. He appeared to apologize for not allowing me in on this part of his past. How could I be mad when I had kept secrets from him? How brave he was to share the source of his pain, a pain he did nothing to cause but had to live with, nonetheless.

I wept without shame at his heartache. I joined him up on the altar so he knew I supported him.

With great trepidation, he told everyone he had a good life as a child. There was no reason to experience sadness. It was a chemical imbalance only medicine could manage until God intervened.

It was at a young age that Jackson found Jesus. His parents brought him up in the Catholic religion. Jackson attended Catholic schools and was an altar boy at St Mary's. When he went to church with his parents every Sunday, he regularly left feeling sad and filled with guilt. However, on the rare occasions when the priest opened the Bible, that's when Jackson expressed his spirits momentarily lifted!

He was thirteen when he approached Father David and told him about the darkness in his head. The priest had counseled Jackson's parents for years and already knew about his medical diagnosis. Father David was gentle and tenderhearted. He opened his Bible and read to Jackson about a man named Paul and his writings. He explained that Paul suffered for years with "A thorn in his side." Many scholars believed this was referring to Paul's depression. Father David told Jackson that God used this man to redeem the lives of many people, even with this affliction. For the first time he could remember after hearing about this apostle, he felt no guilt or shame at his condition. This priest told my husband he believed Jackson was special and God would use him as a mighty soldier one day.

Jackson prayed with him and he said a miracle happened at that moment. God took away all the pain and unrest in his head. He said it was the first time he had felt whole in years. Jackson continued to have Father David mentor him until his untimely death.

Jackson turned to his people and, with tears streaming down his face, said he hid the past from almost everyone he knew, but he never once forgot what the pain of depression did to his mind and body. A hush grew over the congregation.

Captain Edwards approached him and turned to the people, and said, "This was not a secret to some. It was something a few of us didn't feel comfortable asking you about. We believed when you were ready to share, you would. We did not know the details of your medical diagnosis. There seemed to be this understanding that you related to the sadness and depression that I and some members experienced. We suspected something that a person has no control over touched either you or someone you loved." Jackson grabbed him, and the two grown men held onto one another. Each member came forward to give Jackson a hug.

After that Sunday, he met with a therapist twice a week. As the months passed, she suggested a program that could match him with an emotional support dog. She knew of a dog that had gone through extensive training and was ready to do its job. Jackson politely declined. He felt that someone else needed the animal. He refused the offer, not out of pride, but out of genuine love for others over himself.

Peter and Isaiah came to me one afternoon and put a file down on the table. Our boys had taken it upon themselves to research alternative programs for training a dog to become an emotional support dog. They spent hours and had connected with a woman that gave them invaluable information.

She explained, with the right training and patience, we could teach a dog on our own. I approached Jackson with the wealth of knowledge they accumulated. I had a binder filled with every imaginable detail on support dogs. After he read it and prayed for several days, he wholeheartedly agreed, but with one stipulation. The dog must come from our local Humane Society.

We packed into the SUV that very day. We all hoped we would not come home empty-handed.

Once we pulled up in front of the building, the sounds of excited dogs greeted us in the parking lot. I began contemplating how we could only choose one and would have to leave so many lonely ones behind. Unfortunately, I voiced my concerns out loud. I heard Isaiah let out a loud sigh. I didn't dare look into the rearview mirror at the expression I knew he would have.

Peter thought he could remedy that problem and with a sweet voice said to his father, "Perhaps we could get two dogs: one for you and one for us?"

I allowed myself to glance back at Isaiah. He sat up higher and nodded his head enthusiastically. He even started to high-five Peter until their dad turned around and they saw the look on his face. Shortly after, they both agreed that one dog would satisfy everyone.

We explained to the shelter volunteer why we were in search of a dog. A look of delight appeared on her face when she understood our needs. There was not a question or doubt in her mind when she brought us over to the cage that housed four dogs.

When we entered the rows of cages filled with so many dogs, I grew hesitant again when I looked at the faces of these poor creatures. *Can I do this?* I started to share my fears with my family when one dog stood up on her back paws, and through the thick wire fence, stared in Jackson's direction.

"What's the matter, girl?" Jackson whispered to her. This bold and pudgy dog lay down in complete submission on her belly and then rolled onto her back, her tail never once stopped wagging.

We all looked at her, and I said, "Well, she most certainly picked you, honey!"

She was a four-year-old golden retriever/mix, roaring with the energy of a young puppy. How we loved her and all her silliness. Lilly brought such joy into our lives.

Isaiah enrolled her in the Good Canine Citizen classes. She passed her first test with flying colors. After that, he took her to more training classes to become a registered therapy dog. I remember how sad he was when she failed her first test. Years later, we laughed and laughed when Isaiah repeated the reason for her failure.

It was because of this amazing therapist and the crazy love of Lilly that Jackson returned to his former self. He became an even better preacher knowing he no longer had any secrets to hide.

Lilly. Poor dear girl. Her breathing was becoming more labored and I feared her physical condition was worsening. I looked again at Peter and he put his head down.

"Mom, I'm positive I broke her ribs when we crashed. I was squeezing her hard so she wouldn't catapult into the front and hurt herself. I heard her yelp and her body grew stiff. Now, look at what I've done to her."

"No, Peter, no. You did everything possible to prevent her from being harmed." I knelt over her body. This time, I moved her heavy wet fur back and forth and slowly felt around her chest cavity. She strained at my touch, letting me know her ribs were indeed fractured. I refused to allow this fact to escape my lips. There was nothing I could do for her. These breaks often healed on their own. I knew Peter would carry the unwarranted guilt if he knew the truth. I turned to him and, with the mask that I wore throughout my life put in place, told him she was fine.

This was the mask I learned to take on and off. On one particular day, though, many years ago, it shattered into a million pieces in the kitchen.

In that cheery yellow kitchen. At that moment, it held too much light and brightness. While making breakfast for my family, the disguise wretched free from me. I felt it. That crushing spirit overwhelming me. On certain nights it might roam. Today was different. It detached itself and invaded my heart.

Jackson must have felt the change in the air because he peered up from his Bible. His look revealed it all. He saw the extreme emotion coming out of the depths of my soul and overtaking me.

I did not wish for Jackson to give me an explanation of what he knew from his experiences of dealing with PTSD. I realized he understood what was happening. I could not listen to any words of advice from my husband.

Besides, the dark voices were drowning out the noise of all sounds. I looked at him and saw his mouth moving and him coming closer to me.

I was being taken away from him, the boys and my life. I wanted to sprint right out of that tidy little kitchen, with its uncontaminated inhabitants. It was too late. His calm voice finally reached my mind. He whispered unfathomable words in my ear. My emotions were so high that I wanted to scream in his face, *I am desperate, obliterated, dying!*

Instead, I looked at his sensitive brown eyes and whispered, "You know you can't keep fixing me. You can't keep pretending that everything will be fine." With those words, I might as well have slapped him across his face. I saw the look of despair in his eyes. I realized I had crushed his spirit once again.

All I could hope for, at that moment, was the boys did not hear or notice this stranger in the room. Thank goodness they did not even glance up for a second because they were too busy with their new iPhones. Peter was texting one of his friends. Isaiah had his headphones on, downloading the newest Christian song of the week. For the first time, I felt relieved about allowing them to buy these smartphones they had saved all summer for. Their focus was on the screens in front of them, not on what was happening to their mother. They remained transfixed on their cells until they got a whiff of what was burning in the toaster.

They poked each other and laughed out loud at the blackened toast ruining the coils of the toaster oven. Calmly, Jackson turned the dial to off and unplugged the ruined machine.

Lilly must have thought she would get lucky and eat what no human would ever touch. She scrambled up from under the table and ran over to my side. She looked up at my face and glanced back to the floor. Somehow, she must have sensed my inner desperation. She lay down with a heavy sigh, knowing her tummy would get none of this and would continue to growl at its emptiness.

I heard Peter laugh to Isaiah and say, "Black or burnt, which way would you like your toast served this morning?"

Isaiah chimed right in with, "Neither, kind sir, I will stick to Mom's plain bread."

Peter's voice was loud with laughter. I had to turn away from them. I thought they might try to engage me to join in on their joke. They didn't see; they didn't know. Their eyes and thoughts went back to their cell phones. Once again, their innocence protected.

I knew Jackson could not bear for his boys to see their mother crumbling. He had shielded them from the truth for years. It was not the right time or place for them to know who I was.

Poor Jackson, he looked so old at that moment; it was as if keeping up this pretense was aging him right before my eyes. I saw the weariness on his face, the sadness in his eyes. I realized he could not keep sheltering me from all the storms that raged within my spirit.

Jackson did what he did well by diverting any potential damage to cause infliction upon our sons. He opened his worn wallet. I was silent and immobile when I saw him hand them each a twenty-dollar bill. He told them to hurry before he changed his mind, and to go downtown to the local diner to get breakfast. This was so unlike him to give them money for what we considered an extravagance.

To go out to eat was a luxury we never indulged in. There wasn't any urge for us to spend our money that way. The kids enjoyed bringing their friends over for Wednesday make-your-own-taco nights. To them, it was much more entertaining to stay at home rather than worry about dressing up and leaving the house. Their friends thought it was the best thing ever to hang with us. Not to mention that everyone thought Lilly was the best dog ever. She followed them outside when they were playing football or soccer. Francesca, who was our sweet neighbor friend, held her off the field, as instructed; otherwise, Lilly would sprint across the lawn and chase the ball. Even though this young lady was a powerhouse at all sports, she chose to sit on the sidelines and once the games were over, Francesca would let Lilly loose and everyone cheered her on!

Lilly was the reason Francesca came to our home every day. My boys walked Lilly and took her hiking every chance they got. However, Francesca was the one that paraded Lilly throughout our neighborhood. She tied ribbons in Lilly's fur and brushed her until her coat shone. Lilly would roll around and stand quietly as Francesca lavished her love upon this dog. It was because of this special girl's affection that our dog passed the Therapy Dog Test on the second try. Lilly now held the title of a registered therapy dog.

Today, they couldn't wait to go out for breakfast, though. They glanced at one another. They had plastered smiles on their faces like it was Christmas Day. My sons raced toward the door. Peter said, "I will have no burnt or black toast today, my mom. I will have no plain bread either. But we thank you for always providing us with a warmed cooked meal, even if sometimes it's a tad too warm."

Explosive laughter escaped from both of their mouths. Once again, I turned to the sink and lowered my head. "Love you, Mom. Love you, Dad," they shouted in unison. They never looked back, saw, or knew what was happening to me.

CHAPTER 3

Hearing echoes of continuous wailing, I wished for the calm they exhibited daily in their lives. The pleading from their chattering, pale lips forced each of us to move closer into ourselves. It made me suffer as if my heart would burst wide open. These sounds were so unfamiliar to me.

As babies, they were not big criers. It was a long-standing joke with our parents that they could last several hours without a meal or a diaper change. Our sons were the easiest infants that existed. So independent and peaceful.

One afternoon, I invited my neighbor, who also was a part of my support system, over for lunch. It was during a severe snowstorm. While attempting to bundle up her toddlers, I heard them howling from their home across the street. They wailed for their mom to acknowledge them. With no response from her, they'd find a way to get their sibling's attention. They made each other cry (or cause their mother to lament) from the minute they strolled out their front door until they appeared in ours.

I tried so hard not to chuckle at the commotion that appeared to accompany them wherever they went. They navigated across the road for their once-a-week-to-sustain-my-sanity visits (as Lauren told me). She insisted no matter what mood her daughters were in, she'd always welcome my invitations. The time at my home was therapeutic for her.

Her daughters' ages were one and two years older than Peter, yet their temperaments were so different from my sons. Lauren marveled how mine amused themselves for hours in the playpen. I hated to inform her they only required each other's company to keep themselves amused. She did not understand how well they played in this tiny space; how independent of me they were. Never had she experienced a whimper out of my two.

Lauren glanced at her girls and declared, "Look at them. I love my daughters to pieces, but wow, how they test my patience! I believe they make up plots on how to terrorize one another. Ryan and I have read every imaginable parenting book and attended numerous seminars. We have not been able to succeed on how to get them to obey, even at their ages of four and five; they never listen." With pure love and exhaustion in her voice, she continued. "They begin this from the minute they wake and persist 'til bedtime. I devote every hour of the day, into the night, being a referee."

Sometimes we both laughed at their antics, but at other instances, she'd grab my hand, with tears in her eyes, pleading for Jackson to pray for her. After she left, I promptly called my husband to appeal for specific prayers for my dear friend.

At various times when I thought of her, I pondered her compliments on my babies and our parenting. I never accepted her or anyone else's expression of admiration, believing it had little or nothing to do with my mothering skills. Instead, they were special babies. They had been this way since the day they were born.

My dad used to banter with me. "Do you recall one of our many arguments, where I poked my finger in your face? Telling you I could not wait until you married and had children? I hoped you'd have two with the same amount of passion as you have!" He shook his head when he said, "I wanted you to understand my frustration on raising such a determined child. Well, now look what happened. Who'd have guessed you got two children, but neither of them took after your defiant ways!"

The amusing thing about these conversations was that my father never recognized the strong will of Isaiah's personality. Both my parents never admitted to any negative behaviors from either of my sons; completely blinded by their love for these boys.

However, my father often reminded me of our conflicts. When he told me, "As rough as it was to raise you, you turned into such an amazing lady." My father voiced some negative words, but afterward, there was always kindness and a hug.

He'd repeat many times how happy he was that I was his daughter and his friend.

I had to twist away from him before he noticed the tears welling in my eyes. I struggled not to dwell on how he never saw the true me; no one did.

Our boys acted as if they were twins, except they were born from different mothers and were sixteen months apart! There was a bond between them that was extraordinary. From the first time we brought Isaiah home, they became inseparable. Isaiah's presence fascinated Peter. Peter mimicked his younger brothers' waking and sleeping routine. Even trying to get us to give him his milk in a baby bottle!

One of the most challenging times we had with them was when they were toddlers. We struggled to get them to sleep in their own beds, and concocted a unique approach getting them to slumber. Several nights out of the week, this was a simple task that passed without incidence. Other evenings, it appeared hours dragged on by reading books or telling them stories to make them doze. Exhausted from this pleasurable, yet tiring task, we retreated to our bedroom once they shut their eyes. Nine times out of ten, when we woke the next morning, they were sleeping together.

When a year went by and none of this changed, Jackson gave in and assembled bunk beds in Peter's bedroom. I rolled my eyes when Jackson reported he wasn't letting them win because he got the upstairs office he'd always desired. I struggled not to giggle in his face because he had a sheepish grin. His smile stemmed from the knowledge that deep down he knew I recognized the truth. The absolute reason was not that he was giving in to them or that he preferred an office upstairs. It was that I could not bear to watch or listen to my babies in any distress or discomfort. That's the way he was, protecting me from everything that might injure or disturb my happiness.

Those two did not appear to notice anybody else around them. The exception to this was Jackson himself. The minute they heard his voice coming in the door, they'd stand in their playpen and squeal with delight. Their tiny little arms reached for their daddy, as he swooped toward them to receive both into his firm arms.

When they learned to walk, I swear they had built-in clocks. They'd smudge the windows as they pressed their tiny noses against the pane. If Jackson worked late, they'd pace the floor until they saw their daddy's truck roll up the driveway. In unison, a recital of "*Da da! Da da!*" would ensue, resounding in music permeating the air! That was the most articulate and passionate they grew throughout their entire day.

Peter formed sentences early in his life, while Isaiah spoke few words until he was two and a half. There was a secret language that only they understood. We observed in astonishment when Isaiah asked for something from us. Jackson would glance at me, asking, "What?" In the interim, Peter would hand his brother whatever it was he was begging for from us!

They matured into young men that challenged Jackson by their many questions, yet always sought his opinions. The older they grew, the more their emotions and responses became sensitive and acute. Peter was stoic. He checked his feelings and carried them inside until he was ready to communicate. He rarely invited us into his thoughts or burdens. We'd notice something massive had emerged when his barriers came down. We agreed not to probe because when he was ready to announce the origin of his discomfort or his joy; he opened up to one of us.

Isaiah allowed his sentiments to flow without effort. There were many thoughts in his heart he'd shared with Jackson and me, and was never embarrassed to admit what he was pondering or feeling. Isaiah was not a big crier, but the injustices of the world moved him. He managed not to shed tears for himself, but for exploited individuals. My sons' personalities were both so different, I was so relieved for this. I claimed to most of my friends that there was no way I could handle two Peters or two Isaiahs!

They rarely expressed negative emotions of rage, bitterness, heartache, or envy. The one silent sentiment they shared in their spirits was a loss in their hearts. They had experienced heartache since the time they were born. What should have been Jackson's and my happiest day was theirs and their birth mothers' saddest.

I innocently took them from the bond they experienced for nine months with moms who loved them unconditionally. Thrust into our lives; into the arms of two strangers. I was ill-qualified to aid them in coping with this loss. How could I realize that forever etched in their tiny hearts were a mother's voice and her smell? I never understood why, for their first few months, they took longer to bond with me. My voice was not the same one lulling them to sleep in the womb. I was not the sound and smell that protected them in safety for their first nine months.

Consumed with wanting children, looking back, I did not comprehend the entire biological attachment. There was a deep connection they shared with their other mothers. I wanted them to have a link to their past. It was naivety not comprehending it. My eagerness to love them and be their mom outweighed any logic in considering this bond.

I felt the need to defend them from this loss throughout most of their youth. These forfeitures were part of the reason I considered them to be special. Once that realization settled in, I became thankful instead of saturated with guilt.

When I was in their birth moms' presence, I recognized that much of their temperament framed in their mothers' womb. It was a bond they shared and would have for all their remaining days. It produced stability and freedom in my life to appreciate the devotion they received at birth. This was what had formed and filled their hearts. The awareness of this afforded me a massive appreciation toward their birth mothers. They not only presented us with the gift of life but cherished their children. Both mothers gave existence to their unborn babies instead of choosing the alternative in ending them.

After many seasons of not becoming pregnant, Jackson came home with a pamphlet from an adoption agency. We had never discussed adoption, and it was a relief he brought up the subject. I should have understood, the minute the last set of experts we consulted advised us we might never conceive, Jackson's choice would be to adopt a baby. It thrilled me he was ready to put the infertility treatments and heartaches behind us. I desired to continue with my life, trusting tiny, jubilant voices could obliterate the years of angry ones.

Many birth mothers and several birth fathers read the bios we supplied to the adoption agency. While completing the paperwork, we thought nothing of checking off each box. There was never a question that we could embrace a baby no matter what color, nationality or disability. Several times, particular people challenged us at the agency, questioning if we read that numerous adoptees might have medical and emotional challenges. Jackson's reaction never changed during these conversations. He would say, "If you were familiar with Anna and me, you'd understand our love is unconditional. We are eager to cherish a child, any of them would be a blessing."

Jackson always had a rough time keeping our personal lives from the public. He bubbled with enthusiasm for our good news. He used to wink and suggest to me, "I should use this as a theme in my next sermon. What do you think?" I pretended not to hear him. But he was persistent.

He was stirring his coffee while his elation filled up the room. His constant whistling was annoying. Jackson continued until I glanced up from my iPad. He begged me, asking if he could share with the congregation how we would be adding a new family member to our lives.

"Definitely not," I asserted. I listed the reasons I was not ready to tell anyone. "My parents have not been told what is proceeding with the adoption. We have kept this our secret for months now. Besides, the agencies said it might be several years before we have a baby placed in our home." If I were to be honest, the true reason was, it worried me that a birth mother might not choose us, or I should say me.

Although he did not agree with my decision, as always, he honored my feelings.

When a year passed, I grew more and more discouraged with the entire adoption experience. He told me one day he realized why we were waiting so long through this procedure.

"God has the baby He meant for us. That little one's lingering, waiting their turn to be born." He winked at me and his tenderness faded my fears and frustration. I couldn't help but laugh after he suggested this.

Later that evening, when I reflected on what he asserted, I snuck up behind him, gave him a tight squeeze and warned him, "You better tell God to hustle on this! I am not getting any younger waiting on Him to arrange for that baby to be in our home." Jackson's rebuttal was always the same. With his undeniable belief, it always was in God's timing, anyhow!

After several more months came and went, he approached me, further imploring me to please let him share with the people. His thought process was that they would know what to pray for. How could I turn him down any longer?

The very next day, after he made the big announcement in church, Jackson got a message on his cell phone. Peter's birth mother chose us from hundreds of home studies and resumes. She informed the agency that Jackson would be the "perfect" father to raise her boy. The interviewer also relayed his biological mom thought I would be a proper mother because my picture looked as if there was something missing in me. She told them she had this intense suspicion I required a baby to love me.

After many months of planning for the baby to arrive, we received a call that Peter's mom had given birth. When we faced her at the hospital, she placed her tiny boy, with tender love and care, in Jackson's arms. Her eyes brimmed with tenderness and tears as she told us, "Now my heart will heal." She glanced over at me and whispered, "I pray that you will heal now as well." How I loved this woman's courage to carry a child in her womb and then lovingly part with him.

The length of Isaiah's adoption was the total opposite of Peter's. Jackson and I recognized several months after Peter's second birthday we wished for him not to be an only child.

We telephoned the agency, and the next day we got a voice message informing us they were in contact with a birth mother. This young lady requested a family with a solid faith. The birth mother grew up in a family of atheists and yearned for believers to surround her child.

Jackson grabbed me and spun me around in a crazy wild dance! Peter giggled, having no clue, but joined in by hanging unto my dress with laughter and excitement.

"Well now, I suppose there's no protesting God's timing on this one, huh, Anna?" His infectious smile crowded out any uncertainty I was thinking.

That warmth did not linger because we received another call shortly after the first one. The attorney relayed the birth mother had voiced concern when she looked at the last pictures we had sent over at her request that morning. She said in my photo there was a hesitancy in my eyes, a haunting look she could not explain. I did not say a word to Jackson that evening. I went up to bed early with feelings of dread.

The next day, I gathered all my courage and called the agency to set up a private meeting with Isaiah's mother. I refused to let Jackson in on this arrangement. If I did not convince her, I would wear that coat of shame for the rest of our marriage. It would turn into another failure added to my growing list.

During that long drawn out morning, while I prepared to meet her, I repeated out loud, "I am a good person, I am loved..." I hadn't realized that Peter was awake in his bed. He called out to me.

When I approached his little starter bed, he said, "Good Mama. Good Mama, I love you. I took him in my arms and felt his love beating inside my chest. I realized then if there were no other children, he was everything I needed.

I met her with new confidence in my being. I could not explain to anyone the encounter we had in that conference room. It was as if two wounded souls merged into a complete understanding. Looking into each other's eyes, there were no reasons to speak. The meeting lasted less than ten minutes. It ended with her signing the paperwork. We both wept tears of pain and joy.

Less than a month later, Isaiah's birth mother, who had an overflowing abundance of grace and love, handed us her newborn son. She tried to hold back her tears. My heart ached for this angel on earth.

As we parted, she spoke in a hushed whisper to her son. "Now go, my little one, fill the earth with your greatness."

We all agreed that both adoptions would be open ones. I remember the barrage of frantic questions from our friends, asking us: "Don't you fear that their mothers would want them back?" and "What if your children want to go live with them when they grow older?"

Although their probes were honest ones, they held no truth in our lives. My children's minds and hearts embellished the words I spoke to them daily: "The more people in this world who love you the better off you will be. Love is the bond we share."

Oh, how they received love from their other mothers! Birthdays and holidays spent with both their biological family and our family. It always felt natural for Jackson and me to welcome them into our home. How could we deny them seeing their babies grow into these fine young men? I am not saying it was easy for their moms. I am sure they missed them when they returned to their own homes. However, both told me it comforted them to see the young men they had become.

When the boys were still young, at my uncertain moments, I wished they had grown inside of me. It was still painful to remember how much Jackson and I had longed for babies before the adoption. Many years of testing and doctors took a toll on our relationship. It was hard to understand when the doctors said physically there was nothing wrong with either of us. How ashamed I felt after each new doctor shook his or her head and said, "Give it time." Jackson would always leave the consultations with such optimism. My head was heavy; I could not raise it from the sadness after these appointments.

While we had tried to conceive for several years, most of my girlfriends became pregnant. I attended so many baby showers, but finally had to decline any new invitations. Even after the first several ones, I left the parties with a sense of loneliness and desperation. Jackson would always be ready to drive me home and try to soothe away my emptiness. He, too, was struggling. Although Jackson, being the rock that he was, kept most of this pain away from me. Infertility robbed us of many years of happiness.

Many more years of losses and love in my sons' lives shaped their hearts. These sorrows and devotion gave them the power to overcome so many adversities.

Our little blonde, curly-haired, blue-eyed daughter, laughter echoed throughout our home when she came home to live with us at three months old. We never met her birth mother. We read in the police report that they found Catherine in an alley in New York City. She wailed above the noise of the city. A Good Samaritan heard her cry and brought her to the local emergency room.

This adoption differed from others. The boys had mothers who went on every prenatal appointment. They were big and strong from the moment they entered this world. This child's future was uncertain from the moment of conception until she was born.

Catherine was withdrawing from heroin when she came into existence. I fell in love the moment I saw her frail little fingers open and close, grasping at the nothingness of life. From then on, I vowed she would live in safety with us and nothing or no one could ever harm her again.

In the first few days, the hospital did not allow us to hold or love her until she thrived. Her poor little feet convulsed in agony. The doctors told us they had no way of determining the extent of the damage inflicted upon this innocent child. They suggested we might take on years of intense caregiving. One even had the nerve to insinuate, "Anyhow, she might not live much longer." His careless words and aloof demeanor angered our family. How dare they play God? I refused to believe any of them. In my mind, I never doubted this child would not only survive her current condition, but someday she'd shine with brilliance. Our family had enough love to lavish on her that any lasting effects of the drugs would vanish.

When we brought her home, she was a robust and chubby three-month-old. No one could believe this was the same weak and sick baby that had tubes hooked to her little frame and monitors pinging just a few months earlier. Her light began changing me. Dull colors became vibrant again.

Jackson and the boys were crazy-in-love with Catherine. I would catch Jackson rocking her and singing love songs in her ear. Isaiah kept telling her he was her protector like Peter was to him. Peter glanced at her every second he got and a smile as bright as the sun shone on his face. Everyone agreed she was the most gorgeous baby girl ever born. We could never imagine what our lives were like before she came into them.

And then it happened. Gone forever…

There was no way of knowing on the evening she passed she would not wake up in the morning. The night I placed her in her crib, she smiled and moved her little hands, radiating happiness and good health. We thought we had done everything possible so nothing could harm her.

But on that fateful night, SIDS (sudden infant death syndrome) robbed us of our baby girl. I grieved for so many years that it became a part of who I was. No family, and especially a mother, can ever prepare for this loss. There were no textbooks written on how to cope with the appalling death of a child. My dreams and desires died with my little baby.

I loved my boys, but it was my deepest wish to raise a girl. They had a man bond that did not include me. I longed for this baby so she and I could do all girly things together. I believed she would come to embody all that was good in this world. I felt foolishly that I could redeem myself by raising a girl. On the day she died, a part of me died, too, never regaining the ability to really laugh again.

I blamed myself for her death and every single second after it happened. So many well-intentioned people with kind words tried to comfort me. The harder they pushed to give me advice, the more I withdrew from their world. None of them had lost a child. Thinking their words comforted me, instead, they had the opposite effect. How could I agree with people who said God needed my daughter more than I did? How dare they tell me this was God's will for her life?

It was only my dear friend, Stephanie, who gave me comfort. This sweet lady brought meals for my family. Stephanie would call first and ask permission to come over before entering our home. She put the meal on the table and then sat by my bed (or wherever I was laying). My friend would hold my hand or massage my back. She never tried to explain away the death of my daughter. Her silence and peace were the only comforts I felt. She sat and let me talk when I was ready to speak. When I cried, she cried, when I yelled how unfair it was, she stroked my arm and said, "You are right." Many months passed, and she gave up many moments of her life to sit with me in my grief. I will forever remember the love I felt when she was in the room.

Something strange occurred when the boys left one summer for a mission trip. That was when the unbearable oppression of grief left my body. I tried to understand what changed on that day. How and why did I awaken from my despair? I learned the truth when they came home from their trip. At the exact moment I arose from the dead, Peter was praying with an African preacher for my life. Peter had shared the story of my loss with a close pastor from the church they were rebuilding. Pastor William Banks raised his hands and cried out to his mighty God to heal my heart.

Peter enthusiastically recounted the story to Jackson and me. He said Pastor Banks raised his arms and there was a supernatural electrical charge that radiated from his hands. This shock went into Peter's hands and rested in his heart. The pastor declared that the power of the Holy Spirit had restored me to my former self. Peter loved to tell this story. His faith had given him the courage to seek a mending of my heart.

After that loss, there were many years of our parents' declining health. We always had a loving relationship with both sets of parents. I cherished Jackson's parents like they were mine; the same was true in his relationship with my mother and father.

It was well known how much Jackson respected my family. Unknowingly to me, Jackson had invited my mom and dad to dinner. My husband was an old-fashioned man and asked them both for their blessings on our marriage. Jackson loved to tell the story of how my dad looked him straight in the eyes and said, "No." Jackson said he broke into profuse sweating, thinking, *Now what?* He said he looked over at my mom for guidance. She winked and said, "You are the best person who has ever been in our daughter's life. We want you as a son!" My dad broke out into a smile and told Jackson the one thing he would need to do was to get used to our family's sense of humor! It did not take long for Jackson to not only accept this humor, but also to mimic it.

We were fortunate to have both sets of parents with us at the end of their lives. Our sons never said it out loud, but I believe it took a toll on them. They accepted new roles of caring for their grandparents. I never asked them to aid us. Both Jackson and I realized our parents living with us meant that it would require all our attention. Since I did not work outside the home, I accepted that I was to be their main caretaker. But, with the enormous help from my husband and sons, there were many hours I was alone in my thoughts.

In the beginning, I prepared everything and everyone for what needed to occur.

Peter and Isaiah would take it upon themselves to help me with all the tasks I couldn't handle. It was their nature to think nothing of lifting my dad off the bed and onto a chair by the window. Their grandfather did not even have to tell them he longed for the sunlight to warm his cancer-ravaged body. Every day, one of them wheeled him into our garden so he could warm his shrinking body. How I cried at the sight of them holding his hand and whispering in his ear. My sons adored him. They had spent many years fishing, hiking, and sleeping over at their grandparents' home in the country. Both were equally as loving to my mom. They never grew frustrated when she called them Jackson, or at other times asked who they were. They both took turns at mealtime, feeding her when she could no longer understand the purpose of a spoon.

Jackson's parents cherished their grandchildren. It was amazing to see the bond they shared even at the end of their lives. Peter gave up spending time with friends and extracurricular activities to love on them. Isaiah sat in their room, holding their hands and spent most of his days praying over them. Both sons wanted to make sure they spent as much time as they could with their dying grandparents.

As grievous as all this was, they grew stronger because of it. Over time, they were more stable and overcame more adversities than one could imagine. How did all this inner strength emerge? What made them stand taller and more robust than any of their friends? Jackson used to joke that if they were any more confident, we would have to build a bigger home to house their heads! As self-assured as they were, there was also an air of humbleness in their hearts. They were the first ones to volunteer on the teen mission trips. Peter would wake Isaiah up early in the morning after a major snowstorm to shovel our elderly neighbor's driveway with no one asking them.

I could count on one hand how many times we had to discipline our children. One of Jackson and Peter's biggest arguments was when Peter insisted on getting a tattoo of a cross on his forearm. He told his father that all his friends were going to the tattoo parlor the next day. He needed his father's permission since he was underage.

The way my husband handled it, Peter might as well have told him he'd rebel for the rest of his life. I had to turn my head, remembering all my rebellious ways at that age. Jackson was not a legalist. The way he acted toward Peter's announcement surprised me. When he grew calm, Jackson explained he was not against tattoos, but insisted he believed Peter wanted this only because his friends were getting one. He said if Peter desired a tattoo, they could discuss it another time. Peter kept silent throughout Jackson's talk.

Isaiah must have been listening to this debate in the other room. He walked into the family room. Jackson was not facing him, so he could not see what his other son was doing. I was not paying attention to Isaiah because I was concentrating on Peter's reaction. When I heard the snickering coming from him, I glanced in his direction.

Isaiah had taken a black Sharpie and drawn a cross on his own arm. He held it up so Peter could see it. He said out loud, "Peter, my brother, save your money and your time. I believe I am as artistic as they come and can do this for you at no charge!" I watched as Peter lunged at his brother until Jackson stepped in his way. Jackson put his lips together to contain the laughter at Isaiah's words. Peter was unamused by his brother's antics and his father's lack of seriousness.

When Peter stormed out the room, I recognized by the look on his face—this conversation was far from over.

The next day Peter walked into our home with two friends who were brandishing their colorful tattoos. I held my breath, hoping he was not disobedient to his father. I glanced at him, trying to read his thoughts. He smiled at me in the way that only he could do. "Mom, Dad was right. If I'm living in your home, I will follow your rules, but on the day I move out, that's the day I'll be showing you my new tat!" His face showed no malice, no disappointment, it was a matter-of-fact look that explained it all.

To think that day may never come. Both sons might never experience college, falling in love, and raising a family. I may never become a grandmother to their little babies. How I dreamed of this after having no more babies in my arms.

Stop! I couldn't think this way. We were alive, and the three of us were together. Jackson was not here, but the way he lived his life was the legacy his children would always embrace.

The sky was getting lighter with the approach of daylight. They needed to save their strength for living now, not for what would never be. As I held them, I rocked them as if they were babies. Neither broke from my embrace for several moments. Our bodies tangled together on the bottom of the raft. How could I tell them the truth? But the longer I allowed them to have hope, the deeper their hurt would be. They finally saw the desperation in my eyes. The knowledge of what happened to their father invaded their minds.

"Oh no, no, no," Peter cried out. "Mom, what happened? Where is he? Are you sure he's dead? Did you see his body?"

I knew I had to tell them the truth of what happened to their father. Slowly and deliberately I chose the words, admitting I had accidentally caused Jackson's death. I needed them to understand he died to save us. He might still be alive if he had not gone back into the plane to release the bins. I wasn't trying to divert the blame of my actions, but they needed to know, perhaps for the last time, he really and truly was a hero.

With a force of anger in his voice, Isaiah yelled at me, "Why Dad? Why was it him and not you? It should have been you! If Dad had let you drown, then he would be here. Did you see his body? I will not believe he is not somewhere out there. And where are the bins anyway?"

I nodded, and Peter spoke to Isaiah. "We need to let Dad go. I can see Dad right now having a conniption because of the way you are talking to Mom in that tone. He wanted us to be strong and brave. How many times did he tell us not to fear? We must take care of our mom. She is not the enemy. Why are you acting this way? I realize you're in shock, but you love Mom as much as you did Dad. He's gone, he's dead, he's never coming back. It can't be her fault. She loved him even more than we did."

With those words, Isaiah turned and flung himself out of the rubber raft. Isaiah's words stung my heart. I tried to follow him into the ocean. Instead, Peter pushed me to the floor, and I sank hard knowing what Isaiah said was the truth. God should have spared Jackson, not me.

Peter dove right in the ocean after him. Lilly was on the edge, ready to plunge in. Her tail was wagging and I am sure she wanted this to be a fun game wrestling her boys. She knew nothing in her heart but love for her family. I grabbed her collar and held on, telling her, "Not now, Lilly, not now." There was flailing and yelling, and bodies twisting back and forth. Isaiah's strength (or lack of it) was no match for Peters.

Isaiah had disliked competitive sports since he was a toddler. When the sports season began, and we announced it was time to go to practice, he would lay flat on the floor. He would find every imaginable excuse not to go to his practices or games. "I'm tired. I have a stomachache. I have homework to do." Our son would beg his father not to take him because he hated being on those fields.

Little Isaiah was not a natural at sports. The last soccer game we ever made him play, he performed so horribly; he made his team lose! It was then I protested to Jackson I would not watch these pitiful sports any longer. "Why should we put in the effort cheering him on when he wants no part of this? We are not doing this for him. You are forcing your hopes and dreams onto this poor boy. It's wrong! We aren't being fair, wanting this more than he does!"

This was hard for him to accept. Jackson so wanted Isaiah to play sports the way he had in school. Jackson felt these healthy competitions were such an important outlet for kids at this age.

After our talk, Jackson apologized to Isaiah. He told him he was proud of him no matter what he did or didn't do. After realizing his son was unhappy, Jackson withdrew him from every sport. Peter would always kid Isaiah and say, "If Mom and Dad hadn't removed you, the league would have taken you out for your poor performance!"

Peter had a well-toned, muscular body. His form was due to spending countless hours at the local YMCA. His goal was always to be strong and healthy: vanity was not the reason he worked out. Peter exercised because he was literally a human shield for many of the weaker students in their school. He took it upon himself to let the bullies be aware if they picked on anyone, they had to come for him first.

I thought back to when he became a defender of the frail. Wasn't it only yesterday Isaiah had struggled off the bus? Just from his gait alone, I understood there was something wrong. When he pulled his cap down even further over his face, I pulled it off his head. A huge welt was forming over his right eye.

"What happened?" I cried out to him as he tried to grab his hat back.

"It's nothing, Mom, drop it, okay?"

Didn't he know me well enough to realize I would never let it go? At the moment, I utilized my deep breathing exercises, although very unsuccessfully. After two minutes of silence from Isaiah, I shouted, "Who and what did this to you?"

Isaiah did not say a word and stared straight ahead.

I immediately thought of Jackson. Was he to blame for always telling him to turn the other cheek? Had he made our son into a bigger target for the bullies on the bus? Why had I not spoken up and disagreed with Jackson? We should have allowed him to defend himself. I wondered if it was too late for him to understand this was a mistake. How could we both be so naïve? I thought everyone liked Isaiah and no one would pick on him, much less start a physical fight.

Peter came into the room, singing from the top of his lungs, but stopped after he looked at me, then to Isaiah, and back to me. I saw the fury in his eyes. His voice was menacing and filled with a deep, intense outrage. "What happened to him, Mom?" I had to step back and distance myself from the anger rising in him and filling the air. It was so unlike him to be this mad. I recognized no matter what I or Isaiah would tell him, he'd avenge all guilty parties to defend his baby brother.

By the time I answered Peter, Isaiah had scampered up to his room and without a sound (as if I wouldn't notice he was not in the room) shut his bedroom door. Peter's anger appeared to be diminishing. Although knowing Peter, until he resolved what they did to his brother, he would let no one have any peace, us included.

He loudly bounded up the steps, two at a time, and entered his brother's room. Isaiah would tell him everything. They allowed no secrets in their relationship. The truth would come out and Peter would defend his brother from his tormentors.

I phoned Jackson to forewarn him of the afternoon's happenings. I could sense the heaviness in his voice.

"I will pray for wisdom," he said. "Do you need me to come home?"

"No."

I hung up, lost again, never understanding what my role was in this. I did what I did when I had no answers. I started…

Peter clomped down hard on the stairs and, without a word or glance in my direction, slammed the screen door shut. I did not know where he was going, but I could not stop him.

Hours later, he appeared in the room where his father was waiting. I could not make out their words. Peter only told me there was no need to worry about Isaiah's safety any longer. There would be no more bullies taunting him.

Jackson never filled me in on the details. He often kept these things from me. I was okay with that. I understood, in his mind, that it was always his way of protecting me. They were only trying to shield me from more hurt in my life. I often wondered if he supported Peter's actions or if he gave him a stern lecture on why two wrongs don't make a right. Either way, I was glad Peter had put an end to the bullying of Isaiah.

Frantic movements in the water brought my focus back to my sons. I could not bear one more moment of seeing them fight against each other. They never battled like this. I disliked feeling as if I was in the middle and them battling over something no one could control.

I did not give any thought to the danger of leaving the raft unattended and jumped into the choppy waters. Lilly appeared confused and frightened. This faithful dog always felt the need to protect her family. With a loud grunt, she plunged into the sea next to me and paddled around, barking at each of us. I tread water, trying not to exhaust myself. "*Stop!*" I yelled. "Come back, you two."

With that last word, I gulped a mouthful of salty water that gushed out of my nose and mouth. I choked and Peter grabbed my arm and yelled, "Get back to the raft!" I tried to ignore his words, but his huge and angry voice was demanding. I had no energy to stay afloat. I complied knowing, I, once again, was of no use to anyone.

I used all the rest of my strength to get our dog back onto the raft. There was no way she could use the boarding straps hanging on the side. With all my might, I leaned over and pulled her into the raft. She trembled and groaned loudly, flopped down and closed her eyes. My heart knew if she continued to use this kind of energy she would die soon. I leaned down on her and soothingly told her to rest.

Meanwhile, I heard Peter yelling at his brother. "You are wrong! Mom needs to live. You understand why, but do you want to die? Do you want your life to have no meaning? You will commit suicide if you stay out here. I will be right here with you. I won't let you go. So, my death will be on your soul. I love you, brother."

Isaiah was pale and weak. He recognized he was no match for Peter. He allowed Peter to grab him by the arm. I heard one last howl of defeat as Isaiah gave way to physical and mental exhaustion. Peter guided him back into the raft, back into life.

CHAPTER 4

Life was so unpredictable, so uncertain. One fact was unmistakable: we had to choose life. Surviving was our only choice. We had to agree to remain strong for each other and for Jackson's memory.

I shifted to Peter and inhaled. Everyone frequently commented on how he resembled Jackson. Now that his dad had perished, Peter's presence was a constant reminder of their father. It was uncanny how Peter resembled him, and Isaiah's appearance was like mine. Strangers often noted how they looked like us. No one could guess they were both adopted.

I exhaled and forced myself to guard my words carefully. I must try to convince them how we can apply our skills to survive without Jackson.

"You both must use your gifts to preserve our lives. Peter, you are in charge; you are now the head of our family. Dad would want it this way. I know you will make every effort to keep us safe. Your father knew how powerful you were in emergencies; how you solved problems with ease. He told everyone you were so levelheaded and not prone to being overwhelmed. Every person who knows our family regularly say you were born to be a leader, like your father. You took control when he was unavailable. At school, you showed another strong trait in your physical strength. You were the most dominant player on any team and awarded several medals for your achievements. At home, we gave you tasks that required stamina. It was fascinating to see how you swung an ax to cut the firewood to warm our home in the winters. You held the furniture up and out of the way so I could clean underneath. Any chore that required heavy lifting, we assigned to you."

"Isaiah, your role has changed as well. Without fail, you were impatient to learn the hows and whys of everything in life. The one who asked a million and one questions throughout the day, that kid who drove us insane with the inquiries. You listened and took it in. Your brain is full of more useful facts than anyone I know. You have a knack for solving problems. Remember the knowledge your father gave you? You surpassed him with every detail you learned. He used to tell me that you were brilliant. Most of the instructors wanted you in the gifted classes, but you resisted at first. That is until you realized some of your friends were gaining more knowledge than you! You were so competitive in school. Now, you can use the power of your mind to keep us intact, to help get us rescued."

Isaiah was still far away in the raft's corner, whimpering. He clutched tightly onto Lilly's fur like a fearful little boy while she tried to lick every tear from his face.

"Stop talking, Mom," Isaiah sobbed. "You're going on and on. Like we care about any of what used to be. Don't you understand? No one will rescue us. There's no chance that we can survive this! We might as well ask God to take us now before we have to suffer for days without food or water."

In all the years of his life, he was the most optimistic one of our family, the one filled with an abundance of hope. It shocked me to hear his words, even though I knew he was speaking the truth. Isaiah appeared to be reaching hysteria again. I had to gain control. "If you need to cry, that's fine, get it out now. We cannot afford to exhibit any kind of weakness out here. We must save our energy for living. There is no turning back or looking back. The could've, should've, would've are gone."

I hated the distant, commanding tone in my voice. I knew I had no choice; he had to snap out of his approaching hysteria. Instead of calming him, my words had the opposite effect. He turned farther away from me and allowed the expanse to grow deeper into himself. He hugged his knees harder into his chest and wailed even louder.

He looked at me with such anger in his eyes. "Our dad is not lost; he cannot be. Dad is invincible. You got so many things wrong over the years. I bet he's out there somewhere. I cannot believe you; you are a liar. You've never been honest with us. No one can trust you. Peter, make her stop. We can't take it any longer. It's not fair how he constantly shielded her, and now she is not protecting him! Lies, lies!" He spat viciously in my direction.

How often had I heard those two words before? Why did they catch me off guard now? But they did. I wasn't prepared to hear the accusations coming out of my son's mouth. I thought I hid my secrets from him and his brother.

From the depths of my being, an uncontrollable fury raged in my head. I shook him as hard as my strength would allow. I was about to strike him, but Peter stopped me from inflicting any further pain upon Isaiah. I yelled at him to shut up. "Do not say another word." Lilly, who had never growled at any of us, let out a powerful and ominous sound at the outrage in my voice. I did not realize how uncontrolled my emotions had become. There was a rage that was bubbling up from the inside; anger I never imagined could live in me.

Throughout my sons' lives, I never laid a hand on either of them. I do not even remember a time that I yelled with such violence in my voice. I hated myself.

The buried anger I had for myself, and everyone who hurt me, I now aimed at my innocent son. I saw fear and shock on both their faces. I was out of control. I could not believe I was going to put my hands on him for anything other than love.

I forced myself to think of Jackson and his unflappable demeanor. Filled with shame that my sons had witnessed me like this, I begged him for forgiveness. He grew silent. He must think I am a monster.

He had every right to retaliate against me. I thought he would rise and lash back. Instead, he moved from his space and grabbed my hand. He kept saying, "I am so worried and scared; Dad would know what we should do."

"You are correct," I told him, stroking his tear-stained face, "but Dad is no longer with us. We only have each other to rely on."

Peter cried out. "No, Mom, we have God. We've always had God. He is the one we can trust. He will keep us safe and alive until we get rescued." Oh, how I wanted to believe his words; I so wanted to believe.

I was considering Peter's courageous statement when I detected something out of the corner of my eye. The fluorescent yellow bins caught my attention as they appeared, bobbing in the sea.

"Peter," I screeched, "our containers!" Up and down in a continuous motion, moving with the waves was one weeks' worth of food. Jackson carefully packed, unpacked and refilled each piece until the supplies fit neatly in their place. We had prepared this food for the starving children in Guyana. However, now we would eat and drink the contents of the bins so we would live. I believed death would not conquer us. It was the first time I had a real glimmer of hope.

Once more, with no hesitation or thought of his own safety, Peter dove into the icy ocean. Lilly seemed to have understood we were no longer playing games. She laid down, heaving a loud heavy sigh, and never once took her eyes off "her boy." It amazed me, watching Peter. His movement in the water so calculated, so powerful, it was as if Jackson had come alive in him. I watched his meticulous strokes reach one prize! Isaiah was so excited he fell backward, nearly landing on top of poor Lilly. She looked so desperate to retrieve with Peter, so

Isaiah remained in the place he had fallen to grip her tightly.

Peter returned with one of the floatable bins. He heaved it onto the side and Isaiah rose and pulled with his entire strength to get it into the raft. I continued to cheer him on but saw exhaustion creeping into his body. Swimming to get another bin was not as easy. He had sprinted to get the first, and now, his energy was waning. The waves were pounding furiously against his weak body. With every stroke, he tried frantically to reach it, but it disappeared over another cresting wave. I watched him stop swimming to tread water.

"Peter," I yelled, "come back! Let me try. Your body is giving out. Let them go. It's not worth losing you! Please."

Just when I thought he could go no further, I heard his voice. His sweet cry, sobbing to the Lord. I listened to his melodious words, so soft and pure. He begged God for the strength to continue. He stopped his treading and floated on his back. As the waves washed over his body, his voice grew stronger while he continued to praise God. Tears streamed down my face as I listened to his peaceful expressions to his savior. His faith—nothing would ever shatter it, not even facing his own death would diminish his love for Jesus. Oh, how I admired who he was.

Knowing how exhausted he had become; I could not believe what I was witnessing. He angled back onto his abdomen and swam forward with a purpose. It was as if he had an electrical charge. His movements were even greater than before he had prayed. I have heard stories of people achieving superhuman power. How a person could flip a car over just using the adrenaline that surged through their body. I never understood how it could happen until I saw this phenomenon in my son. With that superhuman strength, he hauled our second bin onto the raft.

For the first time since the accident, we hugged and dared to laugh. For one second, it felt like former times. We almost forgot that Jackson was not there to give the "quadruple" bear hug he was so famous for. I grabbed them and held them tighter than I ever had.

How Jackson must be weeping tears in heaven, knowing we would live. I told them, "We will make it and rescue will find us. I thought I heard Daddy give out our coordinates." I wanted to believe we would survive. They both hugged me tightly. Their hearts beat furiously in their bodies. With those beats, I knew I had to force myself to believe my own words.

We opened the bins. The first one contained Bibles and books for the church in Guyana. With determination and also a sense of guilt, I did not hesitate and quickly threw out everything that this bin contained. Peter nodded in agreement as if he understood why I was doing this. Isaiah had a look of pure anger on his face. "I'm sorry, Isaiah, but there's no way we can have this extra weight on the raft."

We excitedly opened the second one, which held clothing.

"Guys, did you know about this bin? I thought we had only enough money to buy the necessities for the Guyanese?"

"Our church donated money weeks ago. Dad had us go shopping for this to surprise you. He hated how upset you were about not having more money because of the raft," Isaiah said.

Peter yelled, "No, no, this isn't the container I thought it was. This can't be. There's no way we left anything behind. The other bin has to be out there somewhere. It's the one that held the food and water for the children! How are we ever going to find it, though? I don't think I have any strength left to get in the water. Maybe it's with the airplane?"

In a fit of fury, he started throwing the clothes from the bin overboard.

"Peter, stop!" I yelled. "Stop! Some of our clothes are torn; we need to shield our bodies from the sun. We can use these clothes for ourselves now!"

Peter's rage continued, and he refused to listen or cease his destructive acts. He persisted until he heard Isaiah's loud crying, but by then he had finished casting away most of the clothes. His face distorted with dread and resentment when he stared straight at Isaiah and shrieked at him. "How many cases containing the water and food did you count?"

"Hold on, Peter! Another bin could be out there. Calm down!" I yelled at him.

Isaiah looked away and gazed out to the sea. His lips moved, but we could hear no sound.

Peter would not let it rest and questioned him again. "You saw Dad or me carry three bins on, didn't you, Isaiah? You remember, you didn't forget, did you?"

Isaiah started wailing. "I thought I counted everything. When we got to Nassau to refuel and Mom and Dad went to the bathroom, I looked back at the cargo. I knew then I must have missed one bin in the storage area at the hangar at Teterboro. I figured I would tell you when we got to Guyana. I knew everyone would be so disappointed in me. I was planning on using my savings to buy food and water once we got there."

Peter shook his head. "How many times did Dad tell you taking inventory in your head was not the same as physically writing down all the stuff that was coming aboard? That was your one and only job on this trip! How could you have messed it up? We will starve to death unless someone finds us and it's your fault!"

Isaiah raked his fingernails over his arms, drawing blood. "Stop this!" I shouted. "It's over. Nothing you can do or say, Peter, will change what happened. I know you're sick and exhausted. Isaiah made a mistake. It would be like blaming Dad for the plane going down. Neither of these things is anyone's fault. Your brother feels sick over this!"

Peter kept shaking his head, but I could see his anger was subsiding. He would not look directly at Isaiah. Instead, his gaze was on the horizon. Softly, he said, "You're right, Mom. I'm really afraid now." He reached over to his brother. I knew his heart was melting and he would not hold on to his unforgiveness,

Tiny droplets of blood dripped onto Peter's arm. Peter's voice shook with anguish. "Forgive me, Isaiah." It was my responsibility to carry the bulkiest things onto the plane. I must have missed it somehow. It is not all your fault. I take responsibility for not paying better attention. None of us can judge each other for any of this."

Hours passed and our first day at sea was almost over. There were no words to speak. Lilly dozed beside Isaiah, who still clung to her. Her breathing had changed little. Both sons shifted their bodies to stare out in various directions. Looking and believing in the darkness that we would soon go home.

The silence between us was almost as intense as the crashing waves. An unspeakable heaviness surrounded us now. I felt we needed to talk about something positive. I would not allow them to hold on to despair.

"Isaiah, tell us again about the first time you took Lilly for her therapy testing."

Peter must have understood what I was doing and coaxed him on as well.

Isaiah cleared his throat. "Lilly failed because her handler, meaning me, forgot to give the most basic of commands. I was so nervous. The kid before me, his name was Devin, he did everything with perfection. He was young, too. Devin knew exactly what to do and say, and his dog passed the test with flying colors. So here I am, thinking I got this under control. I'm a lot older than that kid is. If he passed, I know we will, too! Besides, Lilly is the smartest and best dog ever. Everyone knew that. Well, I guess I was a little too cocky. When it was our turn, I remember I kinda puffed my chest out in pride. You know the way Peter consistently does? Instead of telling her to leave it when the tester dropped those treats on the floor, I said, 'Get it!' Our ever-hungry dog ran so hard to get the food she knocked the lady onto the floor. Luckily, no one was hurt, but she failed Lilly. I was the one who messed up. Good old Lilly didn't care, though; she got those extra treats! Failing the therapy test is something you never let me live down, did you Peter?"

Peter laughed. "Yup. Every time a piece of food fell on

the floor in our kitchen, I'd say to you, 'Should we tell Lilly to get it or leave it?'" A bit of sadness lingered in the air. Peter glanced over at his brother, and proclaimed, "I'm sorry for the times I busted on you. I should have been a nicer brother to you."

Isaiah shook his head. "Aww, Pete, you are the best brother ever."

That shared memory and those sweet words helped ease the panic that was rising within me again.

"That is a great memory, guys, one I could hear over and over. I'd love to listen to more, but I am exhausted I think I might collapse. We need to take turns getting rest."

I looked at them. Peter was stiff and trembled uncontrollably from physical exhaustion. I knew he could no longer stay awake. I was wary to ask Isaiah to be in charge, but it was time to rely on him. I could not question whether he could handle this crisis. We all had a role to play, and I had to trust he would be up to his part. I wanted so much to be the one to stay awake, but I had become too weak, physically and emotionally.

"Isaiah, would you be the first one to watch for rescuers?" I could tell he was relieved and proud I had chosen him to be in charge.

"I promise I won't mess up this time, Mom." He put his fingers to his forehead and with a slight smile, Isaiah proudly announced, "Aye aye, Captain, first mate is reporting for duty."

As tired as he was, Peter couldn't help but laugh at his brother's antics. "No, you are the captain in charge now. I just promoted you myself!"

Isaiah winked, and I was glad that his sense of humor had

returned and he appeared to be almost back to his normal self. Well, at least as normal as he could, considering the circumstances.

I found a spot to lay down. It caused even more pain in my back when I drew my knees into my chest, but I had to allow them to have as much room as possible. I couldn't stop thinking about how we took for granted the luxuries we lived with. We had everything, and yet I often complained that our towels were too old, or we needed this or that. I vowed that when we got home, I would never complain again about having to make a bed or clean the house.

Peter, who could barely kneel in place any longer, came crashing down so hard the raft seemed like it was about to flip over.

Isaiah's eyes looked like they would bulge from his head. He kept saying, "Easy, Peter, easy."

Although I ached and there were no comfortable positions, before I knew it, I was asleep.

Then the dream began. It was a beautiful, sun-filled Sunday. The smell of the lilac tree filled the house with its strong perfume. I loved the spring. Everything that was dead was now alive and fresh. It was a time for renewal, a time for a rebirth. I sang the latest "Casting Crowns" song. Everything was perfect in life. Not a single thing could dampen my mood. I baked my family's favorite meal. Easter was a celebration and our favorite holiday. Nothing could prevent us from observing this momentous occasion. I would surprise them with my special lemon meringue pie. My stomach was giddy with anticipation of what tonight would bring. The sun's warmth was fading along with the afternoon light.

Our sons were in the yard for most of the afternoon, hanging out with friends. Jackson lay down on the couch to take a nap after the third church service. I called out to them that dinner was ready. I heard their laughter and chatter before I walked into the dining room. I turned the corner and there they were. All three of my men looked as handsome and happy as ever. I glanced at each of them, waiting for one of their usual jokes.

"Looks great, Mom. Did you make it, or was that the grocery store's van we saw dropping off the dinner?" I smiled at the same remark they had made since they were little children.

It started when I had overcooked and undercooked an entire dinner. To be honest, though, it wasn't just that one meal when they were younger. At that particular supper, Jackson smiled and ate it because he told everyone he appreciated a home-cooked meal. Really, it was because he never wanted to hurt my feelings. The meals got better after that disastrous one, but the boys never let me forget it.

As I stood over the table, I glanced up at the oval antique mirror hanging above Jackson's head. I was expecting to see my reflection, hoping I looked as excited as I felt. I wanted everyone to see how happy I was. Instead, the woman looking back at me was a stranger. An unknown face, smiling! It was me, but it was not me! She wore a mask covering my face, another woman's mask over my own. Panic rose in me. This unknown woman sat and placed her hands on my children while Jackson gave the blessing.

"God bless Anna for being a woman of God and loving Jesus with her entire heart. Amen."

Peter added, "And thank you for giving us a mom that believes… a mom…"

"Mom! Mom, wake up."

I willed myself to focus on where I was and what was happening. However, my dream…actually, my nightmare… would not leave my head. I tried to remind myself that it wasn't real. But the eerie feeling would not leave. My back and neck were so stiff I could barely sit upright.

When I finally glanced upward, I saw they had opened the survival kit and took out the fishing pole. Isaiah leaned so far over the side I was fearful he would fall in. "Be careful," I admonished him, while I watched as he cast the rod out to sea. Before I could even thank them for their efforts, Isaiah whooped and hollered, he had caught something! Cautiously, he pulled the flopping fish toward him. He unhooked the lure and we watched as the fish stopped moving. As hard as that was for me to see, I knew it was what would keep us alive. Before I could speak to them, he caught an even larger one. I realized both my sons would do everything possible for us to survive. I told them how proud I was, how thankful that they were my sons. "It would impress your dad. You have already done so much, to not only keep us alive, but to give us hope."

I was grateful for the years they spent their summers at

Camp for Christ. They learned to build shelters and fish for their meals. This camp had instructed them well on how to live. It taught them how to rely on Christ and not the world. In both ways, they excelled. They loved it there. Each year when June thirtieth rolled around, the air in our home grew lighter. They could hardly wait to see all their friends from camp and get back to that way of life. When they grew too old to enroll, they signed up to be counselors.

Jackson and I looked forward to our time together while they were away. Although we missed them, it was a time we focused on our relationship. Everyone commented we looked like two teenagers while we held hands on our evening walks. We spent late nights around the backyard firepit. Jackson made sure there was plenty of wine and beer in the fridge with the kids out of the house. We could empty ourselves of any title other than husband and wife. I allowed him to sweep me away into his arms, the arms of my soul mate. We danced and laughed, and slept in most mornings. Well, most mornings, until Lilly decided she had to eat and take her walk. Those were some of the finest hours of our marriage. No voices could destroy the inner peace I felt during that time.

We loved the carefree days of summer, but the boys also craved structure. When September sixth came, they got just as excited to be in school. They were so intelligent and excelled in every subject. Isaiah's test scores were higher than Peter's, and we knew Isaiah had a very high IQ. Peter knew it as well. I believe that's why he pushed himself at sports. There was a two-year age difference, but three grades separated them. I was grateful for this span because they were so opposite.

I called them my "night and day" boys. I was happy their teachers or coaches never made comparisons.

The irony was that they were the only ones that measured themselves against each other. There was a healthy rivalry between them. We allowed it to remain because they were the best of friends. It never reached the point of harming either of their self-esteem, so we never intervened in their playful competition. They did not allow their physical and mental differences to impede their relationship. While Peter was an outstanding athlete, Isaiah was the star pupil.

As different as they were from each other, their friends were that way, too. Isaiah's were the nerds because they focused on academics and technology. In my days, that word was an insult, but today those kids with that label knew they were the ones who would get fine jobs after college.

There were many nights that Isaiah was at a friend's house until late in the evening. He enjoyed setting up new computers or cell phones of a friend or their family member. Isaiah loved learning and was thrilled to teach others what he knew. He had patience, understanding, and used his in-depth knowledge of technology to help others. His friend's parents called to thank us for letting him come over to their homes and help. I used to laugh with Jackson and say," "Hmm, did he ever show me or you how to program our phones or computers?" It was bewildering how he took time for others, but for us, he'd grab the phone from our hands; his fingers moving quickly over the screen. He'd hand the phone back to us with a wink and would say, "There, it's done. You can thank me later. I would prefer cash over a credit card."

Peter's friends were the jocks. Many of them played at least one or two sports. They watched most of the New York Yankees' and Buffalo Bills' games together. Sometimes they rented a van and traveled to attend those games. The minor leagues drafted several of Peter's friends. Once he lost interest in sports, Peter followed a different path.

Growing up, they surrounded themselves with friends that were believers and those that weren't. Daily, my sons faced many worldly choices. As far as I knew, they remained faithful to God. They shared such a unique bond because when one became enticed the other remained strong. Temptations were all around in our tiny community. We weren't naïve parents. We recognized drugs, alcohol and sexual relations were pervasive.

Due to Jackson being a minister in our small town, he knew some of their friends had chosen this path. Jackson counseled grief-stricken parents; families whose children were in the throes of addiction. These were the hardest meetings he had. He never complained when asked to visit one of their sons, daughters, mothers, fathers—in jail or a hospital. My husband would call the caregivers as soon as he heard their loved ones were in rehab, or in an emergency room. He had such compassion for all the young and old who suffered from this horrific disease.

Jackson's temper would emerge when he spoke of the laws that were so archaic regarding drug addiction and mental illness. I knew by the loudness of his voice when he was on the phone with an insurance company that denied in-patient treatment for families; he was without fail an advocate for them.

One of Peter's best friends had been in and out of rehab for the last three years. Mark could not fight his demons alone. He constantly reached out to Peter for prayer and companionship. Late-night phone calls, meetings at the local diner, Peter was consistently there for Mark.

Mark's eulogy was the hardest one Jackson ever had to deliver. His voice broke many times when he spoke of the love our family had for this beautiful boy. During the service, Mark's parents came to the altar and put their hands on my shattered husband. Jackson voiced, for the first time in front of his congregation, that he was angry; furious at God for taking this child when his life was just beginning.

I worried about how people would feel about Jackson sharing his personal displeasure in God. The congregation, and everyone from our town, sat still in the pews. I saw and heard a few people exhaling after his angry outburst.

"It's okay to be angry," Jackson told them. "God is mad, too. We live in this broken world that allows such terrible suffering. He knows and understands. We, however, can do something constructive with this rage. We can share Mark's story, hoping it will save one person's life." I never heard Jackson preach with such intensity before. After the service was over, many people told us they finally had peace in their hearts.

Mark was a fine young man who touched everyone's life. He was both the president and class clown. A boy that practically lived at our house from the time they were together in kindergarten until tenth grade. With love and affection, he referred to us as Mom Two and Dad Two. In return, we loved him like our own.

Mark was funny, intelligent, and creative. However, he lost those traits when he became addicted to opiates after a back injury on the football field. It was a freak accident when he and Peter plowed into each other at the first scrimmage of the season. After the impact, Mark's back was so twisted, everyone thought it would paralyze him for life. However, he was a fighter and amazed the staff at our local hospital the day he walked out the door without any aid.

Unbeknownst to us, the pain and the overwhelming sadness of not being able to play sports again led him to self-medicate on marijuana. Peter, alone, carried this burden of knowing but telling no one the trouble his friend was in. It was the way Peter was, loyal to a fault.

Although Mark's parents had some knowledge he was smoking weed, they did not realize the degree of his substance abuse. They forced themselves to smile and tell everyone he was doing fine.

Addiction held such stigma and misinformation, even today. No parent wanted to believe their child was dependent on drugs. Many addicts thought they could get clean on their own. Some uneducated people believed they chose this lifestyle. It took months of education for our family to learn dependence on an illegal or legal substance was not a choice, but a disease. Still, we even had a hard time learning to separate Mark the person, from Mark the addict. It was Peter who showed us we only needed to keep loving Mark, not judging him.

In the beginning, he tried frequently to get Mark to quit. He begged and pleaded and did everything in his power to get him to stop. Toward the end, Peter realized that no matter what he or others wanted for Mark, it was up to his best friend to choose sobriety.

Mark let no one know, other than Peter, that he was actively using each time he left rehab. Mark's mom begged me to find out what her son was on. All I could do was hug her and tell her I would try to get Peter to speak to them. Jackson, Isaiah, and I spent many nights pleading with Peter to let us help his friend. Peter would shake his head and tell us, "Mark is the one who needs to let his family know." Peter knew how bad it was, but I don't think he believed he would lose his best friend to drugs. They thought at that age they were indestructible.

Peter carried incredible guilt. He was the one who walked away with no physical injuries that day on the football field. Although he never voiced it out loud, I believe he felt it should have been him laying on that ground that day. It was after this accident that Peter went to each of his coaches and resigned from all sports. He also withdrew from us and spent more time alone in his bedroom. This frightened us. We knew he was fighting the lies of guilt and shame. The deception of survival guilt.

I spent many days outside his room, pleading for him to let me in, muffling my cries into my hands.

Jackson finally had no choice but to intervene. "Peter, if

you don't come out in five minutes, I will break the door down." It terrified us to think Peter's feelings of hopelessness might cause him to turn to drugs to cope. Jackson hated that he doubted his son's resolve. The fear we both maintained clouded our judgment against him.

Finally, Peter emerged from his bedroom with fury written all over his face. Jackson asked him if he was on anything and told Peter we would get him help. Peter could not believe we did not think he was strong enough. I was very embarrassed about our doubts when Peter sat us down and shook his papers in front of our eyes.

"This is what I have been doing these last few weeks since Mark died," he shouted, as he threw his papers at our feet. "This has kept me sane." In that time we worried over him, we did not realize he was preparing his college essay.

He wrote the story of his best friend. He told the account of how he picked up Mark from his last stay in thirty-day inpatient rehab. There was something different about Mark this time. He said it was not in the words he spoke, but the look that lingered in his eyes. Peter described that there was an awkward silence for most of the ride home until they passed our church. Mark asked Peter to pull the car over. It was then Mark poured his heart out. He told him he could no longer take the pain he had caused so many people these past several years. He said how one night, while he was in rehab, trying to get to sleep, he cried out to Jesus to take away the pain. At that moment, words from *someone* filled his ears.

"At first, it startled me, because I knew I was the only

one awake in the room. Although the voice was soft and gentle, I buried my head under the pillow, hoping it would go away. I realized, though, the sound was not in the room, it was coming from my heart. I've experienced nothing like it before. Suddenly, there was a peace that flowed throughout my body. For the first time in years, I felt whole. I realized it was the Holy Spirit prompting me to surrender my burdens. I knelt on the floor and asked God for forgiveness for what I had done to Him, my family, and friends.

"I wrote you this note. I want to confess everything I've held onto these past years. Here, take it, read it later, I do not want to see my buddy crying in front of me like an overgrown baby," he said. "Drop me off at my house. I have a lot of wasted time I need to make amends for. I want to start with my parents. Maybe you can pick me up tomorrow and see what kind of trouble we cannot get into."

Peter drove away from Mark and knew his friend had received salvation and he would be okay with God by his side. What Mark did not tell him, though, was even as he was beginning a new life with Christ in the center, the misery and constant back pain had not subsided. Mark called his doctor to get an urgent appointment for help with managing his agony. Unfortunately, the person who answered the phone did not give the physician his message. When Mark called back again the office had closed. Mark tried texting Peter to ask if he could take him to the emergency room. Peter was working out at the gym and then went straight to the library. He never checked his phone until later that evening.

In the meantime, Mark could not take the suffering

any longer. He texted a local drug dealer for a few pills of oxycodone. The dealer sold him drugs laced with fentanyl. It killed him instantly. That evening, Mark's parents found him unresponsive. The Narcan that was on his nightstand would remain untouched. He had passed away many hours before.

Peter carried this letter in his wallet and studied it every day. I gasped and sobbed when Jackson took the letter and spoke the words of Peter's dear friend.

Petey, it read, *I know you blame yourself for everything that has gone wrong in my life. I know how hard you tried to save me. I want you to know none of this is your fault. My addiction started way before the accident on the field. I want you to understand that long before that happened, I was dependent on marijuana. You know how everyone is saying you can't get addicted to marijuana? Well, they are wrong. I was an addict way before my injury. I'm pretty sure I wouldn't have progressed as fast as I did to the harder drugs if I hadn't already been smoking weed for years. I had a propensity to fill the void I felt my entire life. Do you remember how I used to have those talks with your dad in his office? I tried for so long to find out from him what my purpose in life was. I struggled hard to find the answers. Your father tried to get me to understand; to know that God had a purpose for my life. I just never believed it until now. You need to realize you were the only one who stayed with me when I was going through this hell. My other so-called friends abandoned me when I needed them the most. Even my family gave up hope on me. My friends and family wanted nothing to do with a drug addict. I never blamed them. I hated who I had become. You and your family were different. No matter how many times I let you down, you tried everything possible to get me help. Even if you told my parents every drug I was doing, it would not have made a difference.*

One of the worst times was when I was with my mom. I remember this like it was yesterday. She wanted me to stop using. She tried everything she could to get me to quit. Unknowingly, she enabled me one day and the next would use tough love. They notified the police, your father, my grandparents, doctors, everyone they could think of to get me help. One day, she had enough of me. I was so high. She caught me nodding off in the foyer while I was trying to remain upright. She was standing two steps up from me. The frustration my mom was feeling gave way to a look of disgust and she announced, "Do you know how hard it is to live with you?" She carried a look of despair with her. I looked down in shame at myself. Gradually I looked up at her and said, "Do you know how hard it is to be me?" I know I broke her heart that day. She hugged me and said she would stop hating me. I told her I would quit that day. That lie lasted until the following morning. Her hurt and pain didn't stop me. I lied and even stole again and again to get my next fix.

I blame you for this: you made me see how futile my life was when I was stealing, lying and doing everything bad to get high. I hated who I had become. You reminded me that there was still a good person inside of me. I want you to know that today when I surrendered my life to Christ it was because I saw how different you and your family are. You guys loved and never judged me. Your home was always open. Yeah, I can hear you whooping and hollering right now from across the road. Thank you for showing me what it means to be full of the Holy Spirit. I wanted it but had too much pride to bend my knee. I can't wait to see what new adventures we will go on together. Hey, I still have time to get into college, maybe we can be roomies? Watch out world if that happens! I love you, bro.

This letter and parts of Mark's life were in Peter's entrance paper. The title was: *The Friend That Only God Could Save.*

Knowing what drugs and alcohol did to innocent lives, Jackson and I understood in our hearts that it could have been our boys taking illegal substances. We understood that dependency on drugs could happen to any member of a family. This disease does not discriminate. Even though we had educated and talked to them about drugs and alcohol, it took only one hit or taste to become an addict. We only hoped that our sons would remain true to what was in their hearts. We never discouraged them from being around these friends and never judged them. Peter often thanked us for not questioning his choice of the people he surrounded himself with.

I was happy he was such a good influence in the lives of others. I would touch his shoulder and tell him I was never perfect growing up. Several times he asked me to reveal my past to him, but I never felt comfortable divulging all my mistakes. Besides, even Jackson did not know all my transgressions. I never lied to him; I just avoided the truth like a plague. I thought when the time was right, I would tell them about everything I had been through. Hopefully, they would understand who I was. I tried to believe they would continue to love me despite the blackness of my heart, a black broken heart.

CHAPTER 5

Mine had shattered so many years ago. How could I know what it was like to be whole and have peace in my heart? I wanted to understand the person I had become; the one who sometimes was now unrecognizable. I hoped to have love, trust, and the unshakable faith like my family treasured. No matter what I did, I never had tranquility. I attempted to do everything right in my life. I wanted so badly to be a good person so I would go to heaven with my family. But Jackson knew. He observed the real me. I could not hide, and he was aware of this deep in his heart.

He, unlike me, never held on to the guilt and shame my decision had caused. Jackson understood forgiveness and grace. He knew believing in these two words you could be set free from torment. With his heart and mind, he had confidence in God's grace. He never struggled as I did. This man could see into the hearts of every life he touched. He believed in the good in everyone, even though he knew of some of the blackness in their lives. In my darkest moments, I questioned this. I wanted to know how he had the ability to see with the eyes of Jesus. Jackson told me everyone had this gift, but few ever chose to use it, and this is how he could continue to love me. Even though I never doubted Jackson's capacity to view *other's* goodness, I will always question how such a kind and loving man stayed married to the "beast" *I* was.

My thoughts shifted when I heard Isaiah's gentle voice in the air. I heard him speaking to Peter, who decided it was Isaiah's turn to now get some sleep.

Speaking to his brother, I could not make out every word, but the tone I understood. Peter's voice grew louder as he told his brother not to fight him about this, it was his turn to get sleep now. Isaiah did not sound tired or ready for slumber. He was never a big sleeper as his brother was, although once asleep it took everything to wake him. Even with the darkening skies overhead, he told Peter he was having a hard time closing his eyes and letting his body and mind rest. Sweet Peter lay down next to his brother, entwined, holding onto each other as Peter prayed over him. When Isaiah still had not closed his eyes, both recalled times from long ago, times, I feared would never be repeated.

They resembled children from the past. Their gentle and calm strengths mirrored the ocean which surrounded us.

I tried to push away the sweet memories of Isaiah as a baby. Thoughts came of rocking him to sleep. Singing soft lullabies as his eyes closed. His tiny body relaxed in my arms. All of this invaded my mind. Those were the greatest moments with my sons. I always felt I received another chance to live by being allowed to love these perfect little beings. It was as if my former sins were nonexistent when I felt their soft little fingers in mine. I was a "regular" mom at those quiet moments during their bedtime. Nothing could touch my heart except for the love that melted it every time they smiled back at me. The accusations had no place in my head when their beautiful hearts beat against mine.

As Isaiah grew older, I cherished the ritual of our late-night talks before he closed his eyes. We spoke about everything that was happening in his life. His thoughts, his feelings, his dreams. He never held back on what he believed in and knew to be true. I was happy even at his age he let me into *his world*. Some nights he would try to question me about my past. He always begged me to share what I was like at his age. It was in those moments I had to turn away and not let him see the tears forming in my eyes. Somehow, he always sensed my despair. He would hold my hand a little tighter and say, "It's okay, Mom. When you want to tell me, you know I will always be here for you." I thought back on how different I was with my parents when I was his age. Letting them in would have led to too much pain. I could never let them see the real me.

Later in his life, when he brought up his childhood, I held my breath. I feared he would admit to remembering bad episodes in his past. Never once did he express any kind of negativity against me. His perception was so different from who I thought I was. His views were only of the good times. During these chats, he often laughed so hard the bed would shake. In the other room, I could hear Peter laughing, too. What joy these boys held in their hearts! Nothing could steal that away from them!

❧

I had to shake my head to remind myself once again everything had changed. Dwelling on the past, even if it was good, might only cause me pain for what was gone forever.

Sitting up, I tried not to invade their conversation. I folded my arms over my legs and drew them deeper into my chest. I swayed with the raft. My eyes closed as I listened to the sweet words tumbling from his lips. Oh, how the beautiful reminiscence of their youth filled the air around our raft. The soft breeze of the night stirred my heart. It held my attention as I listened to their shared memories. I tried to allow my heart to open to their sweet recollections. Now more than ever I needed those thoughts to saturate every part of my being. I wanted to focus on his words and the feelings they stirred in me. However, the feeling of anxiety held me captive by a war dividing my mind. When would it end? There was no quieting the evil that raged in my head and heart any longer.

"Peter, what do you think were the best times of our lives, huh?"

Peter mumbled to his brother, "I don't know; we had so many good times together as a family."

"You know, you remember, come on talk to me, Petey."

Peter grinned and replied, "Too many to list, brother; too

many to even remember. I guess, though, if you're pinning me down, I'd say, it's the time me and my friends were teasing you. We dared you to lick the sign that was in the shape of an ice cream cone at the Country Drive-In. Of course, you did. When Mom found out what happened, she grounded me for a week. Funny, you weren't mad, but boy was she upset with me and Karl!"

"No way, Pete. That wasn't a good time in my life!

"Yeah, you're right, I'm only teasing you like I always did."

"Come on, Pete, humor me now. I need to talk about it. I am getting scared. I keep thinking we will never have any fun in our lives again. I really believe this is the end and we are going to die out here. No one will find our bodies. I miss Dad so much..."

"When I look at you, I sometimes think you are him," Isaiah said. "You always looked so much alike. I was a little jealous of that, you know. I can't believe I just remembered this from such a long time ago. I was so young when this happened. I never told you of the talk I had with Dad. I did not want him to think I was unhappy. I was afraid to tell him how I felt. You know Dad, though, he had this way of making anything that was negative, turn into something that was positive. You never knew about this, but I wanted so much to look like you guys."

"One day I finally told him what I wanted. He held my hand and said, 'Isaiah, touch my ears.' I reached up to touch his ears and he said, 'You want ones like these? No, you don't, no one wants ears like mine. Peter might have them someday, too, if he continues to look like me. Look here,' he said and then made his ears move every which way. I remember giggling at the sight of his ears going to and fro. 'Well,' he said, 'Do you want ears that go back and forth, or do you want nice tiny little ears like your birth mom's?' I told him, 'I want wiggly ears, too!' He laughed and grabbed me as hard as he could and held me up over his head and said, 'Then I will find you some big ears, too!' Dad, always being true to his words, asked me if I wanted to be Dumbo for Halloween that year. It was my favorite costume ever." Peter allowed a laugh to fall from his lips. "Look, Isaiah, do you want wobbly ears still?" He wiggled them until Isaiah was laughing so hard, he developed violent hiccups.

The continuous sound of the wind and waves grew dim until, at last, both the wind and Isaiah grew still.

"Peter, can I tell you now, what we both already know? The best, *the best times* in our life was when we went to the Hughes house on the lake."

Peter's reply was a quiet, "Uh, huh, I know. It was, and now probably always will be."

"Remember how the Hughes family let us stay at their lake house every summer for two weeks? Besides the baseball tickets, this was the only gift Dad allowed his friends/congregation to give us. I'm so glad he loved that place as much as we did! The long ride there, phew, it seemed to take us forever. You always kept telling me to read a book to distract my constant questions of *are we there yet?* Dad always laughed. And then he hummed a song, and we changed the words to make it into a funny joke between the three of us! The ride home was different. You would fall asleep the minute we got into the SUV. Sometimes, I would draw a mustache on your face when you were in a deep sleep. I would stop the minute I saw your hand reach out, ready to swat mine away. At other times, Dad would sing so loud you put your pillow over your head and went back to sleep."

Peter smiled, and Isaiah continued. "I loved those rides home because Dad and I would talk about our future. He listened to everything I had to say. He believed we could do and be anything we wanted. Even when I said I would work in McDonald's—because I loved their French fries and Mom never let us eat fast food. He would nod his head and say 'You do what you want and do it well. We were put here to serve others. So, if serving in a restaurant is what you're called to do, that's awesome!'

"He encouraged us to follow our hearts as long as we seek God's will first. Man, would the ride home go way too quick."

Peter nodded in remembrance. "I wish I had not fallen asleep every time and joined in on your talks. I know Dad never told us what he thought we should do with our lives. I should have told him I wanted to be a doctor in Uganda where our sponsor child was from. I thought if I met this child and his family, I could heal their sicknesses. I kept it a secret all these years from everyone except my guidance counselor, Mrs. Walker. She encouraged me to follow my dream. My grades were pretty good, but she told me with my community involvement I could get into almost any school I applied to."

Out of nowhere, Peter seemed to talk to his dad. "I never told you two days before we left, I got an acceptance letter to McGill University to study medicine. I have the letter folded up in my pocket. I wanted to surprise everyone when we got to Guyana. Now it doesn't matter. I don't think either of us will ever go to college. None of us will ever get to see our dreams come true. How stupid I was to waste so much time because I was afraid to tell anyone. I was scared to leave."

Isaiah looked up and said, "You? You Peter? You could have gone anywhere and done anything you ever wanted. Dad always told us that. Why did you think that way?"

Peter looked over at me, hoping I could not hear. "You know why, Isaiah. One of us had to be with, Mom. We had to be there when Dad was not."

I shifted at these words and gasped out loud.

Isaiah knew I heard Peter, so he changed the subject to their time away from me. "Remember when we used to get ready to leave? Mom never understood how we could pack our bags in less than an hour. She always teased Dad when we brought down our clothes in plastic bags. She looked the other way and shook her head and said, 'They do not get that from me, do they?' Then Dad would say, 'Well, if you let me pack my clothes in a plastic bag then I would, too, so I guess they do take after me in that area!' He would hug her hard and tell her how much he would miss her and her great cooking. He reassured her he always prepared gourmet meals for us at the camp. We would see him wink over her shoulder at that statement.

"Mom always looked strange when we left. I was too young to understand as much as she missed us, there was a relief we were going. It was always us guys, while Mom stayed home and did those "female" things with her friends. Mom called it her vacation, and Dad told us it was our male-bonding time. I always wondered why Mom didn't want to come, too. I never wanted her to feel left out. I knew Mom always put us first, and I thought she wanted to come but didn't want to intrude in our time together. But when we got older, I knew Mom wanted us to be alone with Dad. Not that we didn't want her there, but it was the only time we had Dad to ourselves. No one calling him asking him for favors, no one relying on him for everything. He was just Dad at those times. We didn't have people around putting him on a pedestal. He didn't even seem like a father when we were there. He was free to be himself in front of us. In fact, he acted like a kid, just like one of us!"

"I remember it like it was yesterday. That was the best time of my life. Every night we ate either hotdogs or mac and cheese! It was Lilly's favorite place to be, too! We would fight over who got to sleep with her in our beds! We gave her hotdogs off the sticks from the campfires. Dad would laugh and say to us he was not lying by telling Mom we ate well without her. Because really, good to us was the *junk* food that came out of a box or plastic wrapping. This was our "men's" secret. Mom would have died if she knew we were eating such unhealthy dinners and letting a dog in our beds! How about drinking soda every chance we got and how we would laugh together? We would giggle so hard the soda would come out of our noses. We could never get enough of Dad's jokes and his animated voices. He tried so hard to keep a straight face when he was pretending to *be in control* of us. It made us snicker even harder at the sight of a grown man that acted more like a kid himself than we were!

"Those hot and humid nights, when it was dusk, we would run to the lake and peel most of our clothes off on the dock. You, Dad, and Lilly always beat me until that last year. I will never forget the look on your faces when I sprinted in front of the two of you. You both were so worried about beating each other you forgot I was right behind you!"

Peter let out a loud chuckle, and said, "But we let you win!"

That revelation brought Isaiah to an upright position.

With a sigh, Peter fondly said, "No, I was teasing you, you came in first that time."

Isaiah settled back down, and I saw Peter take hold of his hand.

Isaiah continued on with his memories. "How old were we, Peter?"

Peter thought and said, "You were five and I was almost eight when we first went there. Mom had a stern talk with us when she found out about us swimming with such few clothes on. She told us no more swimming without suits on. We had to put some of our childish ways behind us. We were men now and had to act like it from now on at the camp. Even though there were no neighbors anywhere near us, she still insisted we were too old for this. I wish we could go back, especially to those night plunges into the water. Not self-conscious of anything. Free to do whatever we wanted and not worried about what others would say. No one telling us what to do."

"We should do it again, Peter. We should do it right now! Come on, there's nothing stopping us now. I don't think Mom cares anymore. Besides, she might even let Lilly come in and swim with us,!"

Peter looked strangely at his brother and shook his head. "When we get home, I promise I will take you up to the lake. It will be like old times. But not now, my brother. Don't even think about swimming in the ocean. We need to save our energy. Besides," he said solemnly, "remember there are sharks and other predators in these waters."

Isaiah nodded in agreement. However, there was something strange in his eyes that caught my attention. He tried to raise up from the floor. He looked at Peter and, with a blank look in his eyes, said, "I think I will try, Peter. I will make it to the Hughes camp. I remember where their place was. If we both go now, we can make it there for our mac and cheese dinner. I thought I heard Dad calling and telling us dinner was ready. Come on, Peter, let's be like kids again."

Peter glanced at me as I made a move to reach Isaiah to tell him the truth. I needed to look into his eyes to see how much he was processing. Peter took his little brother's face in his big hands and said, "No, it's not dinnertime yet. We must sleep first. It's time for bed."

Isaiah seemed to respond to his words. Before I could reach Isaiah to ask him what he was thinking, he lay back down and closed his eyes. A small tear formed at the corner of his right eye. He said, as though he was speaking only to himself, "Even if we make it back by swimming there we can't go back. We can never go back. Everything has changed." He stroked Lilly's matted fur for a while until he drifted off to sleep, holding tightly onto her. My heart shattered into tiny pieces once more.

Peter looked up at me and called me to come to the other side of the raft.

"Mom, I'm worried about Isaiah. He's not making sense. He seems to be very confused."

I nodded in agreement and told him Isaiah was experiencing shock. "I took his pulse and it is weak but rapid. His breathing is also very irregular. We need to keep an eye on him at all times. We have to make sure he is the one to get the most fluids."

Peter said he wanted to share something else with me. There was an urgency in his voice that caused even more fear to creep up into my throat. Peter told me he had a vivid nightmare while we both slept, one he could not get out of his head. He said he never recalled any of his past dreams. Terrified of not only the dream but the dread which filled his heart, he said he couldn't stop thinking about it.

Peter reminded me when they were growing up how Grandpa used to interpret dreams. "Isaiah used to have some pretty wild ones. When he got up, he would quickly run to his computer and write them down. He would then email Grandpa. No matter what it was about, he always interpreted them."

I nodded, confirming to him I recalled my father being able to do this.

"Well, Mom, I know I never asked you before, but did you get that gift? Can you do it, too?"

I shook my head. "No."

He looked a little helpless at that point. Before I could stop him, Peter repeated everything he remembered. It was the very same one I had! I froze at his words, not knowing how to respond. He asked me if I knew what it meant. He told me what bothered him the most was how he called the stranger Mom. Should I tell him and make him even more confused by letting him know he had dreamed my nightmare in its entirety? I mentioned none of this to him, not yet. I had to determine what this meant before I revealed the truth to him. I asked him several more questions to discern if he could remember anything more. I knew there was nothing he could add. They were identical in every way. How could this be? I have never, ever heard of two people having the same nightmare in their sleep.

Peter must have sensed something was off with me because he had a fearful look in his eyes. "What, Mom? What are you not telling me now? I have to know what you are thinking."

What could I tell him so fear did not overtake him? I replayed the dream in my head. Where was I? Who was this woman they had called mom and wife? What I recalled, and caused the most dread in me, was when they prayed. They had thanked this woman for her belief. Why had they never thanked me for my beliefs?

I took his hands in mine and, with all the courage I had, I told him I had the same nightmare.

He kept shaking his head in disbelief. "You couldn't, Mom, it's not possible."

"I did, Peter, and I do not understand it either."

He laid his head down on my shoulder. He was six feet two. I was five-foot-three. It took every effort for him to reach down to me. I held him and told him we will figure it out and it should not worry him right now.

"Come on, Mom, this means something. God uses dreams to help His people. Think about it, please. We must find an answer."

I promised him I would try to discern its meaning, even though it was the furthest thing I wanted in my head. I could not lie to him and knew I would have to concentrate more on its meaning.

Another three days passed with no sightings. We had grown weary and hopelessness was setting in. Each of us was having a hard time staying awake in the intense sun. There were loud grumblings from my empty stomach. We caught no fish in the last two days. Lilly seemed to be slipping into a place of uncertainty. There were only a few bottles of water and granola bars left. I knew I would eat no more.

The raft was deflating again due to the heat from the sun. I wondered if Peter or I had strength left to perform the task of manually inflating it with the pump. I started to try to start the procedure but Peter said he could do it this time. I sighed from relief, knowing I was no longer capable of this chore.

Peter broke into my thoughts by yelling the waves were getting rough and we needed to do something or we would lose our possessions. I could hear his voice above the roar of the waves. From nowhere, there was a tremendous shift in the winds and the sea was raging. The water bottle I held onto flipped into the air above our heads and into the choppy waters. Huge swells were around our tiny raft. The sea salt drenched everything in its way. Isaiah was still sleeping. We really were not wrong when we said, once he was asleep, he could sleep through anything. I grabbed him and wedged myself between him and the side. My back was acting like a barrier to prevent the force from knocking him overboard. Although my bones still ached from the crash, I knew I had to support him or I might lose him to the sea. I pushed as hard as I could against the side, while also pushing back into Isaiah. I watched as the waves threatened to not only take our emergency equipment, but to take each of us with its force. I told Isaiah to position himself so he could stay in the raft. He attempted to grasp the oars, the flare, the flashlight and most of our remaining food supply but the force of the swells knocked him to the bottom of the raft. It was too late for Peter or I to even try to grab them. We watched in horror as they vanished. I yelled at him to hold on to my back and not let go. Peter could no longer stand. He squatted, holding desperately onto the side of the raft and onto his dog.

Lilly grew frantic and attempted to brake free emitted a weak and horse yelp. I kept yelling at her, saying, "It's okay." I became worried she would jump overboard. Peter tried with all his might to keep his grip on both his dog and the raft. It was of no use. Lilly could not stand the noise from the crashing of the waves. Another huge wave crested over our raft. This time before any of us could react, the ocean drew her into its belly. I thought for sure my boys would dive in after her. However, shock registered on their faces. It's like they saw it but could not admit it happened. They knew there was nothing they could do. I held onto Isaiah as his eyes grew wide with fear, expecting the worst.

"She's gone, Mom, she's gone." Only left behind were memories of her. "I cannot save her, Mom, I'm too weak to go after her now." Isaiah's fear grew as he grabbed my hand.

I called to him, saying over and over, "You are my baby. I will not let go of you. Lilly is with Daddy now. I bet he is hugging her right now at this very minute. She was meant for him and its time now they should be together. Hold on. Do not let your grip on me loosen. You are strong, you can withstand the waves, do not give up. I've got you." After several minutes, I felt him relax, but it was not because of my words, it was something else.

I glanced over at Peter, with his eyes closed, and saw Isaiah also had shut his eyes. Listening as the two of their lips moved in unison, I could hear their words above the roar of the waves. I knew they were reciting their father's favorite Psalm together—Psalm 23: "Even though I walk through the valley of the shadow of death…" What started out as a silent individual prayer, grew louder and bolder from each of their mouths. When they finished, Peter's voice rose above the crashing waves. "Lord, we know Your will is perfect. We believe You hear our cries for mercy. We trust You, Lord." Before he could add amen, the waves subsided. There was nothing left but the calm sea. Both boys bowed their heads in thanksgiving for this miracle from God.

With the quiet in the air, from the depth of the sea came a sound none of us could ever dream we would hear again. There was Lilly treading water. Her hoarse growl continued while going under and coming up again. Just as she seemed to be submerging for the last time, Isaiah rushed to the side of the raft. He stretched as far as he could to grab onto Lilly to bring her back in. His eyes which just held fear and hopelessness, now were bright with laughter. He held on tight to Lilly. He said to Peter, "Well, I guess you were paying attention to the stories of Peter in the Bible, my brother! You must have been taking lots of notes in Mrs. Sherman's Bible class! Never once did you take your eyes off of Jesus. So glad you didn't falter for a minute! Hey, you should really be like Peter in the Bible and walk on water to find land for us!"

Peter laughed out loud and said, "No, my brother, *we* never took our eyes off Him. And *we* could walk on water although I am sure I would still beat you there!" Their laughter ended when they noticed me standing by myself. Both looked at me at that moment, and I swear I detected a look of regret in their eyes. Peter broke the silence. "You and I, I mean, not *we*," and they both put their heads down in unspoken grief.

I looked away from them and out into the horizon. I knew this time we had been spared. There would not be many more times we could survive in these conditions. Not only was it getting more difficult for us to stand, but we also lacked strength and I knew our rations were depleting. I was at the point of taking almost nothing into my body. I decided, several days ago without their knowledge, we could no longer feed or give Lilly any more food or water. She was barely alive at this point. Falling over the raft used all the energy she had. Her once glorious coat was sparse and matted. I could not even believe she had survived the waves that had cast her overboard. Her tongue was swollen, and her belly bloated. She lay on her side. When we stroked her body, her tail would occasionally thump weakly. I knew it was time to let them know I was no longer feeding her. Telling them that we had to keep the remaining food for ourselves would be one of the hardest things I would ever have to do. I knew they would be mad and blame me if she died. I had to put them first. They knew deep down inside she was dying, but they could not bear the thought she would die like their father.

I was always petite and thin, but now, I was skin and bones. I thought back on the years when I tried so hard not to gain weight. Now I would do anything to have meat on my bones. My pants were hanging off my waist, I had to pull them up around me. My blouse was thread-thin; it felt as if it were two sizes too big. My once long blonde hair, which Jackson loved running his fingers through, was now tangled and knotted. My poor boys had their pants hanging off their bodies. Their worn shirts flapped with the wind. They had little on to protect themselves from the raw elements. Peter's muscles seemed to have disappeared overnight. His physical traits had changed. Looking into their faces, they had such different complexions. It reminded me how everyone always commented Peter had Jackson's skin tone and Isaiah mine. Although Peter shared none of Jackson's genes, he had Jackson's dark complexion. His olive skin now deeply tanned from the hours and days we were adrift. He had those beautiful Greek features, which were a blessing from his birth family. The beautiful bones in his face were more pronounced and no longer lovely. Now, they were a constant reminder of not eating well for the last ten days. I glanced at Isaiah, whose birth family came from Sweden. He shared their gorgeous ivory white skin. We always got sunburned and tried to stay out of the sun. There was no avoiding the intensity of the rays that scorched our bodies. He was red and blistered around his sweet little lips. His light blue eyes sunken into his face. With no hat to cover his blonde hair, I saw the redness and peeling of his scalp. His feet were raw, with open, oozing wounds. However, Isaiah's drastic weight loss got my attention. He had always been on the husky side, while Peter was lean. It troubled me when I saw he had lost more weight than his brother and me. A lot more.

I questioned him on what he had to eat today. He did not answer me. I pressed him again and asked him, "What about yesterday?"

He would not look at me. He turned away from me, and said, "Why don't you ask Peter that same question?"

I was in no mood to explain to him why I was asking him and not Peter. I asked him again, a little more forcefully this time. Isaiah turned toward me with a cold-hearted stare. I knew I had no authority over him any longer. I did not want to continue to argue with him while we were struggling to stay alive. I did not want one bad word to pass from my lips if these were our last days together, but still, I needed answers. I looked at Peter. He looked at Lilly who was now panting so heavily her chest looks like it would break wide open. Oh! I knew now Isaiah had given up eating so Lilly could live longer. Isaiah did not need to tell me when he stopped eating; his weight loss told the truth. I realized he saw I had not been feeding her. All of his portions were going to her now.

Filled with so many emotions about what he had done, how could I be mad at him for doing this? How could I question his motives when he loved our beautiful dog who made everyone smile? Yet, I knew there was no way I would let him sacrifice his life for Lilly's. As much as I loved her, I loved my sons more. I crumbled to the floor in a heap next to our faithful friend. I wept tears of anger and sadness. The guilt I had was holding me down next to her. She must have thought once again she must comfort me in my despair. She tried to rise to her feet and fell with a hard thud on the floor. Her breathing was so labored. I realized now her time was ending. I looked at my sons and told them we needed to let her go; she was only living for us now. I cried and told them to tell her it was okay to go. Both boys rushed over and held onto her and tried to speak those words.

"I don't think I can do it, Mama," Isaiah cried. "I don't think I can let her leave me."

Peter got up and turned his back because his sobs became so intense. He spoke into the air, "I cannot watch, I cannot see her struggle to live.

Isaiah hugged Peter and stood up straight and tall and said he would do it for both of them. He thought Dad needed her now more than we did. As Isaiah brought himself down next to her, he placed his face right into his dying dog. I reminded them she had always known their love for her.

I lay down beside her and whispered to her almost breathless body. "We love you and you did your job always. You do not need to stay here for us any longer. Go find Daddy, tell him we are alive and we will survive."

Her tail gave one last thump, and with her last breath, her spirit departed. I screamed silently in my heart. *Why, oh why, do you take all I love?* I knew this question, along with the others, I held onto would always remain unanswered. Wracked with sorrow, I delivered her to the ocean and watched as she continued out to sea. Finally, she melted into the nothingness of the forbidding ocean, while we drifted away.

CHAPTER 6

Further and further into desolation, another day passed, transporting us toward nothing. Both boys fast asleep, and I was losing my mind, realizing we would never go home. I forced myself to recall the details of my journey in this world, trying with desperation to concentrate on the positives that took place through the stages of my life. But the consistent blackness, that enveloped me before, and now, will be the ruler of my heart.

I stared out into the horizon; my dreams abandoned into the depths of the ocean. Isaiah stirred in his sleep and my focus shifted to him. "Isaiah, wake up. I need to rest. It's your turn to keep watch." Forcing myself to sound like I believed my words, I said, "Maybe you will come across a search team while I sleep. It would certainly be something if you told Peter it was you who got us rescued. I can just picture it, you rubbing it into Peter that you were the real hotshot in the family!"

"Aww, Mom," Isaiah answered, his voice weak. "I never needed to be top dog or have the spotlight on me. I've always known who I was. You heard Peter confess he tried to maintain that image to build himself up. He didn't have half the confidence he displayed. I'm positive that's why he's always had this larger-than-life personality. You know?"

"You're wise, Isaiah. Dad told me that about your brother frequently. I never understood it until now."

Isaiah raised his head. "Can I keep watch from here? I cannot move my body any longer."

A chill flowed through my veins. He knows we will succumb to this sea. "Of course, my little love. Please don't sleep, though. If you can't keep your eyes open, wake me or Peter. You understand, right? No one will think you aren't strong if you need more rest." I watched him closely before I felt confident to let him be the lookout.

"'Kay, Mom, I love you so much."

His comments were continuing, but my eyes were no longer open. It felt as if I had merely shut them for a second when the unnatural motion of the raft and the loud noise in the air awakened me. *What is that? Am I dreaming? Is that the sound of a ship?* I sat upright and glanced up in the sunshine. It was! A rescue ship! Oh, Jesus! We will live!

With all my strength, I shouted, "Here, over here!" Trying so hard not to fall over the edge of the raft, I waved my hands in a pitiful motion to attract their attention.

"Hey, I yelled! We are here!"

The large ship was disappearing. It was going out of view.

"No, no, no! Stop! Please come back!" I was beyond frenzied now. We no longer had our flares left or the paddles with the reflective coating on them to attract the ship's attention. All I could do was continue letting out hoarse shrieks of help.

How did Isaiah let it go by? Why did he not see it? I looked fearfully over at him. He was sound asleep. He had fallen into a deep stupor. The sound of the ship did not exist to him. Even my yelling did not wake him.

But Peter was wide awake. His eyes clouded over with sorrow and resignation. "I must have heard it when you did, Mom. It was too late, though. Don't waste any more energy yelling now. How did you miss it? Why didn't you wake both of us so we all might give it everything we have? Why did you wait 'til it was nearly out of sight before you yelled?"

I had to defend Isaiah for the last time because everyone's tempers had become elevated these past few days. There was no reason for Peter to blame his brother as well.

"Oh, Peter, my eyes grew so heavy, there was no way for me to keep them open any longer. Forgive me."

"I do, Mom. I always have. Everyone, especially God, has always forgiven you. Won't you accept this now, please?" Peter begged.

I turned my head. I would not listen to him for one more moment. When I looked back at Peter, he also had fallen into a deep slumber.

I listened, still hoping the boat would turn around and recover us. Instead of the noise of a ship, the whisper of his voice resonated in my head. my sweet Jackson calling to me. "Remember our love."

What a love it was. For Jackson, it undoubtedly was love at first sight, but it was not the case for me. We met at The University of Albany. I was looking down at my class schedule and map of our campus, searching desperately to find my way through the maze of buildings. I had the worst sense of direction. I used to laugh and say I'd get lost walking out the front door of my home.

Where was Fran? She planned to meet me ten minutes ago at this exact location. This morning, she caught the look of panic on my face when I was trying to memorize where I would be going. Brightly, she proclaimed "Honey, let me be your guide today. I can meet you before our class together." She promised she would not be her normal late-self, and we'd walk to our theology lecture together.

I looked up to see Jackson standing in front of me. It was like he was waiting for me to bump into him, and I did. He laughed and, with a dazzling smile, asked, "Are you lost?"

His words and his presence caught me off guard. "No!" I spoke in a sharp tone. Striving to come across as confident, I spoke a little too loudly: I realized, perhaps a little too late. I watched his smile falter for just one second. Instantaneously, he appeared to regain his confidence.

He shrugged. "Sorry, you looked like you needed someone to help you. I thought maybe I might show you how to get to your classroom."

"Honestly? Do you know where I am going? How can you help me when you don't know my destination? Why do men always assume they know everything about every woman on this earth?"

His smile was mysterious this time. "Oh, but I do."

I rolled my eyes and withdrew my attention from his searching brown eyes.

He turned away and left me. It infuriated me, his cockiness. Geez, I reflected, who does he think he is? How can he pretend to know anything about me? I have to admit, the opposite was true for me regarding knowing him. I learned practically everything about this gorgeous man from all the girl talk in our dormitory. He was the captain of the baseball, football, and lacrosse teams. He was the man every woman wanted to bring home to meet her parents. None of that impressed me. I had always fallen for the bad boys—the kind that would love 'em and leave 'em. That's what I felt I deserved, and normally what I got. Now, in college, though, I had put all the bad boys behind me. Really, I put all men aside to concentrate on my academics. I was through with them. I disliked every man that ever lived other than my dad and my brother. Nothing but pain and heartache had ever come out of any relationship I was ever in.

Just then, my roommate appeared by my side. Fran and I met our freshman year when we both got "stuck" in rooms with girls who were our complete opposites. We ended up spending more time together in each other's dorms than our own because we had so much in common. We bonded over music, books, and movies. Fran and I roomed together from our second semester as freshmen until now. Fran took me in under her wing like a mother hen. She had my back and cared about everything I was experiencing. I kept no secrets from her and trusted her fully. Fran never judged me or made me suffer to feel soiled. She was fun and exciting. Always up for an adventure, yet she recognized her limits. Fran was the most popular girl on campus. Everyone loved her. I never understood what she saw in me.

At first, most women at our school tried to steer away from her. She was so beautiful and outgoing. The jealousy amongst some freshmen ladies was absurd. Once you got to know her, though, there was no doubt she was a good person and you couldn't help but love her. Fran made friends with everyone who crossed her path. Sometimes I had to admit, in the beginning, I was as jealous as some of the other girls in our dorm. I told her one late night while we were out walking on the shore of the river, just how envious I was of her. She would laugh at my honesty and tell me if only I knew how much she wished she was me.

I never understood this until I met her so-called family. They were brutal toward her. Nothing she said or did was ever good enough. They came from wealth as I had never experienced. They were cruel in all their remarks and gestures. She told me after one painful visit, her parents had always wanted a boy. She was a disappointment to them from the day she was born. Nothing she did pleased them. For someone who never felt a family's love before, it was amazing how she gave it away so freely.

When my dad came to visit, Fran melted. She would say do you understand how much I would give to be a daddy's girl? My father treated her extra special because he recognized her wounded spirit. He included her in our family-time when they visited and always invited her to dinner with us. My mom loved her, too. The two of them would laugh at my dad's jokes.

Fran's judgmental tone slightly surprised me when she said, "I overheard everything that just happened. Why are you always so angry, Anna? What is wrong with you? Jackson is one of the nicest and brightest guys in our school. I have been a friend of his since we were in middle school together. He's the real deal. You were way too hard on him and he did not deserve the tongue-lashing you gave. Jackson was trying to help you get to the class. You are always so mad at the world."

Her words sent a dart into my ever-splintered heart. *How do I do this?* I thought. How do I rid myself of the pain and the disappointment that followed me my entire life? I met her kind eyes which showed no sign of judgment, but a deep concern. I said meekly, "Well, he is kinda cute, isn't he?"

She laughed. "The way he looked at you I guess he thinks the same way."

I blushed, not wanting to even speculate about him any longer.

When we finally reached our theology class, much to my shock, there was Jackson. Next to him were two empty seats. I tried, with desperation, to look for any chair not near him. Nothing, except those two empty seats which had his long arms draped over them. He patted the seat he wanted me to sit in. There was nowhere else to go and being so embarrassed by my outburst earlier, I sunk down low in the seat. I practically slid right off of it! Fran and Jackson looked at each other and both burst out laughing. During the entire lecture, he had this huge sweet smile on his face. When Jackson winked at me, I realized my heart would either shatter forever or finally heal after all these years.

It didn't take long to realize healing was occurring the moment I met him. He had an ease and charm like I had never seen in my life. From that day on, he saved us both a seat and after class walked me to my next one. At first, he casually mentioned he did this so I wouldn't get lost. After the first few days, I had the impression, it was because he wanted to be with me as much as I wanted to be with him.

It took four weeks from our initial encounter for him to ask me on a date. I worried at first, he was like every guy I dated, all he wanted was to flirt until I fell hard, but he was different. Jackson was kind and polite, what people refer to as a southern gentleman. He said he waited to ask me out because he felt anxious that I would not accept. How could he not recognize I would have followed him to the moon? I was only waiting for him to ask me to go there with him.

Our first date was what most people would have referred to as a disaster. He picked me up at my dorm. Jackson would not come up to my room, but waited downstairs in the student lounge. Many of the girls whispered Jackson was in the house. Most of these ladies had secret crushes on him. He did not recognize the stir he was making downstairs.

Fran came running up to our room. She said, "If you don't go down there now, five freshmen are waiting to sink their claws into him. You should look at the vultures swarming him like roadkill!"

Fran had no filter on her mouth, so I laughed at her description of the ladies who were dying to be near Jackson.

Instead of rushing, I took my time knowing he was here only for me. It had been the gossip amongst the students we were looking like a couple now. At first, I wondered why he chose me instead of the beautiful, extroverted women on campus. Later, he told me and everyone else that heard about our relationship, he knew the moment we met he wanted to marry me. In fact, he continued even further by saying Fran was the one who told him all about me. Basically, she set me up with him, although neither would admit it, but I suspect him standing in my way was no coincidence at all!

Peter and Isaiah would roll over with laughter when they overheard him say this to others. They had no way of knowing in their young lives what it was like to fall in love at first sight; to trust you found your soulmate. I was glad Peter was cautious about dating. He had taken Rebecca, his childhood best friend out several times to the movies. They both concluded it felt strange to them to be dating when they had been friends for so long. Rebecca's mom, Pam, was extremely disappointed at their lack of connection, but secretly, it relieved Jackson and me. I remembered all the heartache of falling in love at a young age and hoped we could spare him any pain. Isaiah was too young to date. Besides, he showed no interest. He had many friends from school, but we would not allow him to be with one girl alone. We permitted him to go out in groups as friends. Jackson and I agreed he had plenty of time.

When I finally appeared for our first date, he handed me the prettiest calla lilies. He explained the florist sold him these because they were associated with purity and innocence, and this was what he loved most about me. He must have seen the look of trouble in my eyes because, he said, "I am sorry, I assumed you would love them."

I forced myself to smile and said, "I do, I will put them in a vase right now." The thought of him seeing me in this way was a complete distortion of who I was. My lies to him began as I carried the arrangement upstairs into my room and tossed them into the garbage can.

The restaurant he brought me to was the nicest one in our college town. With walls covered with famous people who had dined there, Valente's was a spot every girl wanted to go to. It seemed crazy to me that he had enough money to afford such a fancy place.

I looked at the prices and decided I better order an appetizer for dinner. He shook his head and told the waitress to bring the biggest steaks on the menu. Jackson recognized I was on a tight budget and could hardly afford a meal out.

Once we got to know each other, he shared with me he had been saving up for four weeks to take me there. "If you hadn't agreed to go out on a date with me, then I would have been richer in one way but much poorer in another."

I smiled, knowing I felt the same way.

The food was delicious. He let out the biggest chuckle when I finished everything on my plate. I assumed he was laughing at me. I put my head down, embarrassed I had eaten so much. Realizing my self-consciousness, he swiftly said, "No, no don't be ashamed I loved to watch how much you enjoyed eating!"

I let my guard down at that point and asked him "if we might order our dessert now?"

His laugh was contagious, and everyone turned to smile at us. I realized I was the luckiest lady in the restaurant, possibly even in the world. Not only was he good looking and smart, but he was nice to everyone. He was patient at red lights, long lines, and unfazed by mean people. He would always tell me it was easier to smile than to frown. I realized he was right, but other than when I was with him, I had a hard time smiling. I always felt people were watching me, waiting for me to fall. I do not understand where that belief came from.

Growing up, my parents loved my brother and I well. My mom and dad had extensive educations and were successful in their careers. My dad had a master's degree in divinity. He taught at the local college, and his students adored him. The waiting list to take his classes never ended. He mentored so many young people through the years. Many nights the doorbell would ring and there stood a poor, confused student in need of his advice and wisdom. It was as if he had an open door in our home to all those inquiring minds.

My mom was a writer of historical nonfiction. She wrote under a fictitious name and no one knew of her talents, never wanting to call attention to herself. She felt her kids should have as normal a life as possible. It was always funny to overhear some neighbor or friend ask my mom if she ever wanted to have a career. Many would comment on how exciting it was to be out of the house and contributing. She smiled and winked at us. Only we knew about her other life.

In the summer months, our parents, my brother, and I were free. They would pack us up and visit countries all around the world. The trip that left the biggest imprint on me was when we traveled throughout the Holy Land. My brother and I learned along with my mom about their ancient cultures. It was there my brother announced he wanted to be baptized in the Jordan River. My parents had the right connections, they got him in the water that very week.

Her books were on the bestseller lists for years. She might have become a very wealthy woman. Instead, she chose to anonymously donate every cent she earned to the local women's homeless shelter. Her generosity helped the lives of thousands of needy women.

My parents were a rare couple who still held hands and laughed at each other's jokes. Both were beautiful inside and out. I swear people used to stop and stare at their loveliness. They were an example of what it means to love each other until death do us part.

Because we lived a double life, we didn't have an abundance of materialistic things. My parents appreciated hard work. They insisted we make our own way in this world. I worked at a young age because there were things I felt I had to have. They told me these were not a necessity, if I wanted them, I would have to pay for them. My parents did not even pay for my college tuition. Later, when some of my closest friends found out who my mother was, they often wondered if this upset me? I never understood their questioning. There was so much love given to my brother and I there was no need for any resentment in my life. Deep down, I felt they were right about making us work hard and pay for my own way. This work ethic paid off well for my brother, who became an entrepreneur at a very young age.

We left the restaurant and headed to an outdoor concert. We had been looking forward to tonight for weeks. As soon as we stepped out of his car, a torrential downpour hit us. By the time we got to an empty spot on the lawn, we were soaking wet. U2 started and the crowd moved wildly with every note they played. I wrapped my sweater tighter around me, hoping to have relief from the intense, pouring showers.

Jackson looked so dismayed. I kept thinking, *Why can't I be like all the free spirits in the crowd, laughing and dancing as if the sun was shining.* I was filled with an aching sadness because I knew I would never be the person Jackson deserved in his life. I turned my head so Jackson was not aware of my tears that mingled with the rain.

For the first time since we began dating, he suddenly wrapped his strong arms around my body. He said, "I want you to be happy. I realize how much you wanted to listen to this music, but I am so wet and cold. I just don't want to be here."

I looked up at him and said, "Me too, let's go!" Before he changed his mind, I yelled, "I will beat you to the car!" We raced each other like two kids.

When we finally got to the front seat, we looked like two drowned rats. Jackson looked at me and I at him and all we did was laugh at one another. He placed his fingers tenderly on my chin and lifted my face up to his. "Promise me, promise me right here as long as we are together you will always be honest. You will tell me everything you want and need in our relationship."

How could I lie to him? I realized though, it would be worse if I told him the truth. I looked him straight in the eyes. "I will always be honest with you."

He leaned in so close, I melted into him. Jackson whispered these words would always be the foundation of our relationship. He kissed me in a way no one had ever kissed me. It wasn't the most passionate one I've ever received, but it was as though I felt it was possible I might experience real joy for the first time in my life. A joy that would never fade from my soul. I felt like I was whole. I fell in love with him at that exact moment.

We dated exclusively throughout our first three years of college. Jackson began to talk about our future. I tried several times to explain to him how I felt about myself; how insecure I was. He never let me finish speaking.

Jackson believed in a different person from who I was. He would hush me and say, "Anna, you are the kindest, most caring person I have ever known." He tried to remind me of all the good in me.

Once again, I never told him how I felt, I was too afraid he would leave. I might never bring myself to tell him I was not ready to consider marriage, and maybe I never would. He was so patient and never pushed me to decide until that fateful day.

We had gotten back from a hike in the Adirondacks. I

was preparing a meal for us. Fran and I moved off-campus in our junior year. It was great to no longer be a part of all the "college experience." Both of us wanted to concentrate on our education and part-time jobs. Fran worked many hours. Jackson spent so much time here, and although he never stayed over, his big presence was always in the rooms.

He told me how much he loved me, and said, "You tell me you love me; I want to believe you." He kept repeating. "I just don't understand, is it me? Is this a game for you Anna? It's been three years since we met."

My look must have added fuel to his fire. His voice raised to a level I had never received before. "If you're not ready now, I don't think you ever will be. I want a commitment. I have been saving up for a ring since our first date."

I told him, "I do love you, but I am content with the way things are. We both realized we were not interested in anyone else. We are too young to talk about marriage. Why do we need a piece of paper to prove my faithfulness?"

His anger rose, and there was redness creeping from the back of his neck into his eyes. He said, "Are you serious?" "You don't recognize the real me if you think this way."

His beliefs on marriage were strong. He never hid that from me. I learned he was a virgin. There was no question he would stay that way until he married. We both realized how hard it was to remain pure, but he told me this from the beginning. He thought it wouldn't be an issue.

I yelled back, but deep inside it terrified me he would leave. "You're right, I don't understand how you are this person who is pressuring me into something I am not ready for."

He shook his head and said, "Anna, my love, you will never find out who you are because you do not let anyone into your heart. I have tried to do everything to make you see I will never hurt you. My love for you will never end. Understand I want to be loved the way I love you. You are the person who can love me like this. Listen to me. I have all the time in the world. I promise I will wait for you and give you time. I cannot be around you every day, though. Maybe you will realize how much you want to commit to me. Call me when you are ready. I love you."

Months passed and I had no desire to eat or sleep. I wanted to reach out to Jackson and tell him how much I missed him, but my pride stood in the way. Fran worried about me. Her concern became a burden and so I shut her out of my life too. My response hurt her, but I did not care who I had injured. She avoided me and must have found a new place to stay.

After what felt like an eternity, I called Fran and opened up about my feelings. I told her I was wrong; I loved Jackson and wanted to marry him. I realized I was ready to find him and told her I would beg him to come back if I had to.

The silence on the phone became unbearable. "What's wrong?" I asked. "Please tell me what happened? Is something wrong with Jackson?"

Her voice quivered when she spoke. "I don't know what to say. I will get in touch with him and, we will be right over."

Several hours passed. I heard a car door slam. I got up

from the chair and glanced out the window, hoping I would see my love running to the door. Instead, to my horror, Fran was sobbing, with Jackson embracing her. She looked up at him and his lips brushed her forehead. The pain of shock held me in place. Did I cry out loud? They parted and looked in agony at my face peering through the window.

What happened next will always remain a blur in my mind. I remember Fran opening the door with Jackson trailing close behind her. His head bent so low he could not look me in the eye.

Fran tried to touch my arm, but I withdrew in fury. She began by saying it was a terrible mistake. They had never meant for this to happen. She said both had felt so rejected by me they found solace in each other's arms.

Jackson came forward and pled with me to forgive him. He was crying and said, "It meant nothing to us. I was lonely and weak. I needed to be loved. I knew you always have been the woman for me, I was so wrong."

My words spewed with venom. "You told me you would wait for me! I hate you both knowing it meant nothing to you. The two people I loved the most in my life and yet you both betrayed me. I knew you were too good to be true, Jackson. You are hypocrites. I do not want either of you in my life! Leave!"

They walked to the door. Jackson shook his head as if he pitied me.

"Oh, don't feel sorry for me," I yelled. "I will find my Mr. Right. When I am good and ready, I will commit to him and you will be sorry." I threw a heavy vase at the door and it barely missed his head. I was full of rage and fear that captured my heart and took my breath away.

My parents visited me several times and did everything they could to talk me into coming home. They understood how lost and lonely I had become; how much I changed. I did not eat or sleep well. I was dwindling while the darkness in me was growing. I started on a downward spiral, frequenting bars alone, and drinking to the point of not remembering anything about that night. I continued on seven-day binges that ended with me swearing I would quit, but I wasn't able to. I hated myself and all I had become. The two people, other than my family, who claimed they loved me, were unfaithful to me. I wanted to drown my sorrows in booze and never remember all I lost.

At Christmas, my parents came to pick me up to bring me home for the break. I shocked them by telling them I was quitting school and had gotten a high-paying job. I recognized the look of disappointment creeping into my mother's eyes. I never wanted to dash their hopes. The weight of her sorrow was too much to bear. I made them leave without me. I will never forget the sound of my father's voice pleading with me to come home. It was too late. I had gotten a taste of what it felt like to forget all your pain in a bottle. I no longer recalled any of the good in me and let the bad become my new identity.

I left school. I worked as a bartender in the local pub and was a favorite of all the regulars. I could not wait until my shift ended so I could drink with them so we would all not feel lonely. I laughed with my coworkers as we took bets on who could get high first. I was always the winner. It was one big party every single day and night.

On a stormy evening, a senior from another college in town walked into the bar. I had never seen him there before. He looked at me with such intensity I had to turn from him. He and his buddies ordered rounds for everyone. His smile stirred feelings in me that had buried for months. We talked all night. We did shots together until I couldn't stand unless I was holding on to something. He told me I was the most beautiful woman he had ever met. He put his hand on mine and said he wanted to learn everything about me. I laughed in his face as he reached out to catch me from falling. My manager winked and told me to go home for the night.

I only remember turning the key and leaning back toward this man who I thought would rescue me from my pain. The next morning when I awoke, I was alone and ashamed. I knew he had violated my body. An overwhelming sense of feeling unclean made me lock this memory away into the dark places of my mind. I remained in bed for two straight days.

Fran heard from a mutual friend what happened. She pounded on the door and yelled she would get the police if I did not open it. When I did, I fell into her arms, crying with intensity. She could only hold me until the sobs ended. All the anger I felt toward her disappeared. Fran called my parents and within three hours they had me packed and on the road toward home.

I never confessed to anyone what transpired that night. I told my parents I had enough of that life and I wanted to get help. When three days went by and I was still in bed, my parents came into my room. They were brutal with their honesty. They told me I had to decide if I wanted to keep living like this or get help for my drinking and mental health.

They took me to alcoholic anonymous meetings, and they went to family anonymous meetings. It was painful at first. Withdrawing from alcohol without being in rehab was excruciating for my family to watch. They never abandoned me and trusted I would get well. Their intense love and loyalty filled the void in my heart. They gave me the confidence to go back to college to get my degree in nursing.

During the day I worked at a nursing home. At night, I took online classes. I poured all my energy into making a new life. Although it was one of the hardest times, I was healing. As happy as I felt, though, my heart still ached for Jackson. I dreamed of him, but was too afraid to mention his name.

I felt sick in the late evenings after I had signed off the computer. The nausea lasted all night and into the early morning hours. I was not sleeping, and my mom saw the dark circles under my eyes. She worried I was taking on too much and tried to talk me out of working every day. I hid my health issues as not to concern her. I promised to go see the doctor on my first day off.

True to my word on Wednesday, I had a holiday. I visited our local twenty-four-hour Urgent Care. A doctor I had known most of my life was on call. After the nurse left the room, Doctor Jennings walked in with a look of surprise. It delighted her to see me after all these years. We did the normal catching up on our families and then she got down to business.

She began by doing a routine checkup. I sighed with relief when she said everything appeared to be normal. However, would I mind laying down for her to examine my body? I laughed when I admitted to her I had not seen a doctor since my senior year in high school.

She smiled, but as her hands probed my stomach, she looked a little concerned. She asked me if I felt any difference in my body? I told her I had been gaining weight because of my mom's home-cooked meals for the last month and a half. Doctor Jennings told me to sit up, as she took a seat next to the table. I felt queasy, and the room seemed to close in. She asked me when I had my last period.

I explained to her I was never regular, but I guessed it was about four months ago. I told her I had been irregular for months because of the neglect I imposed on my body. I felt like it was due any day now.

Her eyebrows raised as if to say, *I don't believe you*, but she remained silent.

A burst of nervous laughter escaped me. "I don't know if you're even thinking this, but I cannot be pregnant. It would be impossible."

Then, the dreadful memory of what happened four months ago caused me to sink into thoughts of despair. Doctor Jennings noticed something was wrong, but had to ask me if I would take a pregnancy test.

I nodded. The results came back positive. I wasn't able to

talk. I had no voice to speak. However, the voice of accusation was loud and unmistakable. I had only one choice to make.

Remembering all this made me look to the sky with the recollections of my sins whirling in my mind. The sun was sinking low now.

Jackson loved this time of day/night. He always said during a sunset God was the best artist that existed. He would raise his hands, let out a sigh and say look at His masterpiece-nothing can ever compare to His work of art. How he wanted me to understand the way he looked at it, to open my eyes to the beauty of God's abundant love. Nothing would have made Jackson happier than for me to believe the way he believed. It saddens me Jackson recognized even when he was breathing his last breath, he could not save me.

How peaceful and still the ocean appeared at this moment. I yearned for that peace in my heart, but no matter how hard I tried I could not capture and hold on to any stillness, it always evaded me.

With no one judging me, other than myself, I decided on that fateful day years ago I was doomed. Condemned to a life which would forever separate me from all those whom I loved and all those who had loved me.

I made a despicable decision to kill an innocent life. I placed that act in a dark vault in my soul, never considering it could escape.

A black shadow appeared under our raft. My demons

were closing in on any remaining time I had left on this earth.

Peter stirred and smiled in his sleep. He must have been dreaming of his beautiful life before the crash. He and Isaiah had only ever known the truth of God's love. They had no regrets because they lived with pure hearts. God forgave them of their mistakes because they asked for forgiveness. The way they talked about it; it was an easy decision. They always said they could not comprehend all of God and His workings. However, they knew by accepting Jesus as their savior they had the gift of eternal life. Their salvation was never a question. They did nothing to earn the gift of everlasting life. Jesus had done it all for everyone when He died on the cross.

The intensity of dread overtook me once again. I could no longer hold my head up. I was tired; tired of living a lie to everyone, including myself. I allowed my head to lower itself down deep into my aching arms. I closed my thoughts to all the memories of what was and what would never be again. I knew I deserved what was about to happen, but I would never understand their God would allow my children to die.

CHAPTER 7

Unaware of what day it was, I had lost track of how long we had been on this raft. Time passed in a crushing silence because we had little energy left to speak. We were losing strength. My mind was racing nonstop with jumbled thoughts. Deep inside, a rage was spewing into my being. I had tried unsuccessfully to push it down. I felt it invade every bone. It poured out of my mouth and into the daylight and nighttime. My sons seemed to shrink from my touch, physically fading into the surrounding air. I was turning into a monster, no longer able to push away the hostility buried for years in my heart.

Peter's sweet murmurings from his dream grew into thunderous gasping pleas for air. "Shawn, Shawn, go away. Stop accusing me!"

I urgently tapped him on the shoulder, forcibly causing him to wake up. "What's wrong? Are you going to be sick again?" I demanded. "You need to lean over to the side; let me try to help you this time."

"No, no, no. That's not it, Mom. It's horrific. I can't talk to you or Isaiah about what I've done!" Peter cried.

Isaiah stirred and announced to his brother of all the times they'd been together, now more than ever he needed to talk. "If you can't tell Mom, tell me!"

Peter leaned and dry heaved violently over the side of the raft. He lifted his arm weakly, thinking he needed to wipe the bile from his lips. Repeating over and over now, "It's my fault!"

What can be this agonizing after what we've been through? I thought. *How can he blame himself for anything that happened to us?*

Isaiah's hand rested on Peter's trembling arm. "Please, Peter, stop. You are not to blame for the bins, we went over this days ago, don't you remember?"

"I want to die now. I did this, the accident is my fault." Peter wailed.

I shook my head *no*, but Peter yelled at me, "Stop. You don't understand, you don't know what I did!"

Neither Isaiah nor I had any words of comfort for Peter. We both had no clue why Peter was talking this way.

Silence, once again, grew between us. I would not force him to speak, and neither would his brother.

Peter was sobbing with no release of tears. He convulsed uncontrollably. I would do nothing to comfort him.

"You've got to forgive me, Mom and Isaiah. Before I die, I have to tell you. I can't let you think maybe this was Dad's fault. I realize, Mom, you never blamed him. Isaiah, you probed me yesterday, asking if we crashed because of something our dad did. I told you, 'Of course, not.' How could

I have been so stupid? It was me; it was my negligence that made the plane go down."

"Hush, Peter, hush. There is no blame on anyone in this family," I blurted out, without caring one more minute if I would upset them. "Your God did this to us. According to you, your brother's, and your father's beliefs, He was the only one who could have saved us. I guess He is not so mighty and good after all!"

Isaiah's eyes grew wide with fear, anger, or was it disappointment? I could not tell. I had enough anger in me to temporarily care less about any of my words.

"Your God," I admonished, "the God of mercy and love. Well, if that was true, we would be in Guyana and Dad would be alive."

In desperation, Peter reached over and put his hand over my mouth, hoarsely yelling at me to stop. "This has nothing to do with God. It was me. Listen, I will tell you exactly what caused this plane's engines to die.

"When we stopped in Nassau to refuel," he said in a voice filled with dread, "Dad told me I was in charge. He trusted me to order the fuel. My pride, oh God, my pride. It got in my way again. The line guy was much older than Dad. The name on his badge was Shawn. He looked surprised when he saw me approaching. I was full of myself, thinking, he must be pretty impressed, such a young guy can handle all the details such as refueling a private plane like this one. He asked me if I wanted to add Prist to the fuel. I blanked out. I should have sought out Dad, but I was too cocky, thinking, I might look like an amateur if I don't answer him. I just shook my head and told him, 'No, not this time.' He said something, but I shut him down, telling him I was the pilot-in-training and was well aware of what we needed and did not need." Peter's voice choked and he did not seem capable of speaking any longer.

Thinking hard on what to say to him after my last outburst, but still knowing I no longer cared about sparing their feelings or their beliefs, I repeated, "Not your fault; God's failings again!"

Isaiah shook his head, and murmured softly, "No, Mom. Peter should have told him to put the Prist in the fuel, this all would have been prevented. The water vapor got sucked into the engine. The water in the fuel formed crystals and clogged the fuel filter. No fuel can go through causing the engine to stop. This is why Dad couldn't understand what was happening to the plane. He had no idea."

Peter's head was now in his lap. Isaiah moved closer to his brother. He gently raised his brother's head and told him, "We forgive you."

Peter's eyes searched mine for absolution.

At this moment, I saw my sons, perhaps for the first time in their lives, as imperfect beings. The idols I created them to be, crumbled before my eyes. I turned from Peter. My anger rose in my soul. I wanted to scream at him. As I glimpsed down at the cruel sea that had no heart, my own heartless reflection stared back. I shuddered as I, too, moved further from my sons. Their mistakes had always been innocent and unintentional. Mine were always extremely calculating and selfish. Still, I purposely chose not to forgive him at this moment. I couldn't.

I know now we will perish. The questions I'd always held onto will die with me in this place of death. The time has long gone where I could reveal the answers to my loved ones. Not only would they get no acknowledgment of their questions, but I am afraid I cannot tell my secrets. All my lies and the mysteries of my life will be buried in the ocean that will take our bodies away with it. Now, it no longer mattered.

The food is gone and the water depleted many days ago. Neither Peter nor Isaiah wanted to be the one to drink the last drop of water. They insisted it should be me. I refused, but could not bear to watch who got the last sip. Both cried in each other's arms, knowing there was nothing left. I wonder if we could live for a few more hours. We had no pretense left of someone finding us. When that boat cruised away from us, my hopes died at that moment. I wrestled with thoughts of what Peter and Isaiah needed to do if I died first; I want them to survive. I knew this was unthinkable and as grotesque as it would be to them, I could give them life. I would do anything to help them live.

Isaiah wrapped himself closer to me. It seemed his temperature was boiling, a fever pouring out of him. Lack of fluid was causing his body temperature to overheat. His touch fluttered like a butterfly into my soul.

"Mommy, please, this is not you. You haven't had anything to drink for over six days. Peter and I watched a movie once that showed what happens to people who are dehydrated and starving. Your reality is distorted."

I peered into his kind blue eyes and realized his words and touch were pushing the demons further away from my mind. I grasped his arms, pulling him closer into me, and remembered Jackson's unshakable love.

"You really are your father," I murmured. "Peter, you are, too. I forgive you. You know, it's myself that I cannot forgive. Both of you have become the men your father always knew you would be."

Life was ending for us. Should we even talk about what may happen if no one rescued us soon or if we didn't find land? How could I prepare them for my death, or even worse, theirs? Both had studied biology. They know what would happen to a body that does not take in nutrients or water. How could I look into their eyes and tell them we had less than a few hours left to survive? Should I add to their misery by speaking the words out loud, or allow these thoughts to die along with me?

The ocean was surprisingly calm and the sky void of color. The darkness meant another day was over and Peter and Isaiah had fallen asleep again. I was meant to keep watch, but I, too, needed to close my eyes.

I awakened to the blazing sun aiming down on us and knew another day would give way to another evening. The ache in my swollen joints was beyond any pain I had ever felt. I knew this, too, was a sign of dehydration. I forced my thoughts to travel to Jackson, wondering what he would say to his children. I knew his arms would encapsulate us while saying this life was temporary. Our real home was in heaven and we were travelers in a foreign land, waiting to unite with our Father in paradise. How could I tell them this when I could not say heaven or hell for so many years?

With the release of those words in my thoughts, the voices of darkness cried out my name. "It is time now, Anna. No one can save you any longer. Jackson is dead, and soon your boys will be with him." I covered my ears, trying to lessen the voices in my head, but they grew louder and darker. "We've waited for years. There is nothing good in you. Now you will pay for what you did. You will suffer the consequences of your actions for eternity!"

"Who is this?" I whispered into the darkness. "Why do you continue to haunt me? Even now, I'm dying. I thought you disappeared. Why have you returned? You are not real. You are a voice that belongs in my mind. You can no longer hurt me. There is nothing left to fear."

The voice of accusation hissed louder. "Poor, defeated, Anna. Everyone loved you and wanted you to follow Christ. You would not believe. Hell is real and it is where you will be, with us forever. You belonged to us long before you killed your unborn child and turned your life from all that was true. The truth was something you ran from; never really believing in it. You paraded around, wearing a mask on your face and a veil over your heart. There were many chances for you to trust, but you never sought your own faith. You always doubted you could have faith like Jackson's or your boys'. Now you must know you are one of us."

I shattered the silence with screams I thought were only in my head. However, they covered the darkened skies, piercing into the black starless night.

Startled out of sleep, Peter and Isaiah both cried out in a panicked voice, "Mom!" They grabbed my hands, trying to pry open my fingers clasped to my head. They had little strength left to force my fingers into theirs.

"Mommy," said Isaiah, "Stop, you scared me. I need you not to talk. I cannot think when you scream. I was doing my best to find Daddy. He won't appear if you keep screaming. Please."

I pulled Isaiah closer into my arms. I felt his ribs protruding, poking me as he slumped into me. His mental state had deteriorated like his physical one. He now had regressed into a child. The blackness of the night did not allow me to inspect the faces of either of my children.

In a gentle voice, I said to them, "Lay down now, my babies. Both of you need to sleep."

"Now I lay me down to sleep I pray the Lord my mommy to keep." Peter's voice was weak and quivering.

That's what it sounded like he said, but I couldn't make it out for sure. His speech was slurring.

Without warning, Isaiah sat upright and said, "I'm going swimming, Mommy. I will take Peter with me. We will find Daddy so we can play games now. Dad's waiting for us to come to him. We can go back into the cabin and eat junk food. Peter told me he saw him yesterday. He said Daddy was waving his arms and telling him he was over here. When I looked, I saw him, too! He was on the other side. I told Peter he didn't win this time; I saw Dad first. I even tried to jump into the water, but he held my arm, he hurt my arm he was holding onto it so tightly. Peter kept saying to me, 'Not yet, we must tell Mom we are going swimming.' He said you were sleeping and you would worry if we were not here when you woke up. He made little sense because Mom is never at the cabin. How could we tell you we are going swimming when you are not here?"

I had heard enough. I looked over at him for meaning and then I looked to Peter to make sense of Isaiah's crazed words. I pulled his face as close as I could to mine, his eyes glazed and starting to roll back into his head. "*No,*" I screamed, "don't you dare leave me!"

Peter looked at me and his focus suddenly seemed clear again. He hardly had the strength to hold up his head.

"I love you, Mama," he whispered. His eyes concentrated on me and it seemed he was coming back to life. His breath was shallow, and I could hardly make out his words. I bent my head to put my ear next to his lips. I heard him say, "Don't you know all we ever wanted was for you to know how much we loved you? Why did you have so many secrets those years? Why couldn't you tell us the truth? Sometimes it seemed you were ready to share everything, but then you would go into a distant land."

Isaiah crawled over to him and said, "Shush, my brother. I saw Dad again a little while ago. He was in the raft with us. Didn't you see him or hear him? He told me she's not ready to speak the truth. Dad said soon she will have no reason to hide. The time is coming and she will have to confess everything she kept from everyone."

I tried to understand what was said but my brain was foggy. Somehow, I did not know what was real and what was their imagination. Did they really see Jackson? Was he alive, and I had imagined I saw his body floating by me? Maybe he was an angel pointing us to safety. He always seemed to be so angelic. Maybe he wasn't real, and I made him up all these years.

I had to bring us back to reality. I knew the time of hiding my secrets was over. It was time to be honest with them. I did not want to go one more minute living a lie. They needed to know everything. To understand who I had become. Maybe this might keep them here for a little longer. My confessions could do this. It was time to face the demons I had suppressed for over twenty years. I only hoped it was not too late for them to understand. Our sons deserved to know what had changed me on that fateful day so many years ago. With a gentle tug, I pulled them in as close to me as possible. The stars were now shining overhead. I could see their eyes held no tears.

Like an inextinguishable fire, my heart burned and raced. I could no longer hold back my tears but I didn't have any to shed, I was so dehydrated.

I told them of the burden I carried since I was a little older than Peter was. I never wanted to hide anything from them, yet it was also something I never wanted to reveal. It was my intention to expose the truth someday. However, after so many years passed, I could no longer bear reality.

Peter laid his head on my lap. Isaiah had no strength left to move his head from Peter's shoulder. It looked like his head was barely attached to his body now.

Where would I start, at the beginning or the end? The end was now; it was where we were at this moment. Would it be easier for them to understand why I became the woman and mother I was because of what happened at the beginning?

Before I could think any longer, Peter mumbled, "Hurry, Mom, the time is coming."

I refused to even acknowledge what time he meant. I stroked his head and then moved my hand to Isaiah's matted blonde hair.

"I will not lie to you about your father. He was a good man but not a perfect one. There was a time in our life he made a terrible decision that altered my life forever. Neither of you need to know the details of your father's indiscretions. It cannot change what led me to the fateful choice I made. Please know I do not blame him. The decision I made was my own. Your father never knew. He never found out the truth about what happened. I hid from everyone the horrible details of the evils of my decision."

"Your father begged me several times to tell you about the horrible mistake he made in our relationship. He knew God forgave Him and you would as well. Still, it was a burden he silently held. I never allowed him to speak about it. I refused to acknowledge the depths of his pain to anyone. This is where I know you will hate me, and I wouldn't blame you. I never told your father about the abortion because secretly, I wanted him to believe I was mentally ill because of what he had done, not what I did. I wanted him to suffer the way I had for all those years. The worst part about all of this was that he blamed himself every time I went into the blackness. I justified not being truthful with him because of his deceit.

"Secretly. All those years, a part of me felt he deserved to be punished. I was the one that should do this, not God. I do not know how I could have done this to him. It was pure evil for me to have kept the truth from him. This was my last secret. I thought I would tell him someday, but it was my final betrayal to him. Now, it is too late."

"He loved me; I know he did. However, even your father's love and faith could not heal or repair me. I believed when I married him his goodness, kindness and love would take the burden from my heart. How naïve I was to think he or anyone in this world could build up what was completely torn down so long ago.

"Do you believe me when I tell you I loved him, too? I always thought he loved me only because of my brokenness. You know he was always trying to mend what broke in two. Daddy always had a soft spot in his heart for the defeated, for the lost. That is not true, though. In the end, when he died for us, I knew he loved me unconditionally.

"He must have realized, finally, I was beyond hope. That was why he shielded you from my darkness. Your father had many opportunities to leave me. I will never understand why he stayed. I believe it was because he was an honorable man and tried to do what was right. I also think he stayed with me because he knew deep down, he was in some ways responsible for what I had become. That somehow he had let me down by not being able to right the wrong I had done to my life."

165

I felt Isaiah's head move toward my face. I saw his bony fingers try to reach up, but he could only grab my hair. Much of it was sparse, but in his fingers, some of it hung loosely. The horror on his face made my stomach lurch. I turned away from them. I violently heaved bile over the side of the raft.

"Mom, you are wrong." Peter's cries reached up from the bottom of his soul. He had no strength left, but this sound was eerily strong. "Dad told us about you. They were private things he thought we needed to know." He breathed deep, but all that came out was a gasp for air.

"Peter," I cried, "don't speak, save your breath. We must make it until the sun rises tomorrow."

Peter refused to listen to my words. He kept swallowing and I heard death rattling in his chest. "We never knew what was wrong until the last time when you were at Sunny Meadows. Dad told us everything then. Before that time, we were told you went to be with your brother. None of your friends or ours ever questioned it each time you went away. Dad made it a point to let everyone think you were visiting your brother. Everyone knew you and William were close and you loved to be with him. For years, Dad avoided the truth. He never lied, but found a way so no one knew the details of where you were. Bill lived in the same town as the hospital. I know that's how Dad justified he was not lying to anyone.

"Finally, though, when we got older, he told us he could not pretend any longer. Do you know how much he loved you? Dad never wanted to betray you. He waited for many years to tell us what was happening to you. He wanted us to understand you were not well. He asked us to be strong. He never needed to tell us you never believed the way we did. Many times, he told us we should always treat you kindly and show you the love of Jesus. He didn't need to ask us to act a certain way toward you. We always loved you and wanted to be good to you."

My heart stopped racing, and my head sunk even lower into my chest. I thought I might never hold it up again. I felt my life flowing out of my body and I kept thinking, *I cannot leave them first. They cannot handle another loss in their life.* However, a part of me knew it was the natural and right way to go. I wanted to leave them before they died.

Peter started a slow and steady moan, and I kept telling him what a good son he was. I was close enough to Isaiah to smell death was upon him, too. I had to speak quickly; I had to do this before they were gone. They deserved the full truth, now more than ever.

"My little love, Isaiah, what I will tell you and Peter is a confession of sorts. I will beg you not to hate me as I have hated myself all these years. We are at the end and I want our last moments together to be filled with love and not anger.

"You need to hear about my first and only child born to me. I called her Grace. Many years ago, I made the worst decision of my life. I became pregnant when I was about twenty years old. Only Fran knew about the pregnancy. The baby was not Daddy's. I know if I had told him he would have tried everything possible to stop me. He would have done everything to make sure the baby lived. I never told my parents because of the shame and guilt I felt about what happened that night.

"Fran was the only one who knew. She took me to the abortion clinic and tried to talk me out of it, by saying I would regret it for the rest of my life. She turned out to be such a good friend, and even tried to get me to place the baby up for adoption.

"I wish you could have met her. You would have loved her sense of humor. However, after the abortion, she lost her zest for life. The sparkle and laughter that emulated from her were gone. Instead, her face and body took on an air of despair. Fran's guilt never left her, and she became half of the person I knew her to be. I always tried to comfort her. I never wanted her to feel responsible for my decision. It's sad I blamed your father for what they did to me. However, with Fran, I never condemned her for what happened."

"Fran died tragically, in an automobile accident several months after I had the abortion. She was driving alone when her car spun out of control and hit a tree. They found her cell phone under the seat. The last text she sent was to me. The authorities believed she was texting when she lost control of her vehicle. Her death was ruled an accident.

"Her parents never even contacted me personally. I only found out she was dead because she wouldn't return my texts that night. I called the NYS police in the morning. They asked me to come to their headquarters. The officer ushered me into a dank and noiseless room. I immediately saw a look on one of their faces, and I knew it was bad. Even though they told me it was an accident, I believed even then she took her own life.

"I called her mom and dad to talk to them about the funeral arrangements. They said she was going to be cremated.

They wanted me to go through her belongings. Her mother said they were on their way to board a plane for a business meeting in London. Her father added, 'We always knew nothing good would come of her. I guess we were always right. Please don't try to contact us again. We have closed that chapter in our lives.'

"I hated no one as much as I did them. I went to her apartment with unfathomable anger and dread in my heart. I started packing her possessions with such care. I held up her soft cashmere sweater which was draped casually on the couch and breathed in her essence.

"When I went into her bedroom, it broke my heart even more. She had a picture of the two of us framed on her desk. It was one of the few Jackson had taken during the good times in our relationship. I picked it up and felt an envelope taped to the backside. It was addressed to me. Fran committed suicide. I shook when I read her words, although I did not have to read it to know what she had done. I had known it all along. She blamed the abortion on herself, for what I had done. She never forgave herself for being a part of what happened to me. Once again, I had innocent blood on my hands.

"I told no one about the letter. There was no reason to put disgrace upon her name. I would not give her parents any more satisfaction regarding what they thought of their daughter. I knew the real Fran.

"I need you to hear this. When I found out I was pregnant, I refused to even call it a baby. Until the moment I went into the clinic, I justified it by saying it was not a life yet. This made my decision, at the time, much easier. The workers explained the day before I had the procedure it was not considered human.

"After the abortion, when I awoke from the anesthesia, I was wild with regret. By some error, the staff had not given me enough drugs. I woke too soon. I looked over and saw her remains on a metal tray. I tried to make them give me what was left of her. In my haze of regret, I thought if I could hold her, she would feel my love and return. I never meant to kill her. I believed, once again, in a lie. It was my fault for not wanting to admit the truth, which was right inside me. I refused to consider, until it was too late, that she was a little being.

"I knew what I had done to this innocent life. Now that my womb was empty, I realized this baby was a part of me. I remembered while I was laying there how I had felt its tiny little movements inside of me. I could no longer deny the truth. I knew now it was a human being, and it existed. The body had a form and was viable at that age.

"I became more insistent I wanted to hold her. I lunged with a small amount of strength to fight every person in a white coat. They looked at me like I was crazy. I repeated her name over and over...Grace...Grace. They did not need to tell me; I knew in my heart she was a girl.

"They told me she was dead. I kept saying, 'I killed her. I killed her.' I grabbed ahold of the doctor's arm. His face registered shock; he yelled at me to be quiet. I saw my blood dripping from his hands. He walked away and shook his head, saying, 'What a mess she is. Get her out of here and make her quiet down.'

"There were pools of deep red blood that soaked the sheets on the bed as they tried to tranquilize me. The prick of the needle they forced into my arm to sedate me made me scream even louder until blackness invaded my being.

"After the procedure, Fran took me to a hotel where no one could contact me. It was she who lied for me. My parents kept calling my cell, voicing over and over their concerns. Fran took the calls and told them I had not relapsed as they suspected. She lied and said I needed a little R and R away from everyone and everything. My parents eventually believed because they had no reason not to trust her.

"When I returned home several days later, I kept that vile act of murder a secret from my mom and dad and your father. Guilt and sorrow took over my life. I had committed so many wrongs. My parents believed my mental state was due to my alcoholism. After several months of sinking into a state of nothingness, they delivered me to one of the first of many institutions I would stay in throughout my life. I am thankful to this day for the help and guidance the hospitals provided me. However, it was never enough to make me whole.

"There were times in my life I had true moments of hope and clarity. I know you remember the happy times. Then the menacing voices would fill my head and heart. The strange part was sometimes I did not even remember what I had done. The therapist tried to teach me how to manage the voices, but I could never shut them out completely. Even when I did not audibly hear them, there was always the sense in my being I was condemned.

"On some nights, on some dark and vicious nights, the sounds of evil made me feel as though I was going mad. It was at those black times your father always tried to free me from the savage beasts inside. I am so sorry I could never believe you or your father's truth. I chose to believe the lies time and time again. He did everything he could to get help for me. The worst part is in the end, he knew no one could save me from this destruction. He realized when I turned away from him, I also turned away from his God for the last time."

The stars were fading as the sun rose after my last sentence. I could now make out the expressions on their soft faces. There was no turning from them. I had to meet their gazes. They were sleeping with their eyes wide open. I lifted my eyes to the heavens. In my mind, I cried out to a God I thought had abandoned me so many years ago, *Let them live. Let them live!*

The distant sound of thunder rolled into the silence. How could I protect them from this storm? How could I hold on to their frail bodies when I have nothing left in me? I heard a soft moan and I glanced over at their still bodies. "Are you there? Are you awake?" Both my boys moved their heads in agreement. "Oh, my sweet sons, our time together is growing shorter."

Peter's trembling hand reached over to mine. "You can still believe. It's not too late. God will forgive you if you ask Him."

I would not reveal to Peter I would never believe those words. I could not tell them I knew from the voices in my head I was already doomed. My sigh must have told him what he did not want to hear.

With a small, pleading, audible voice, Isaiah said, "Mommy, it's okay. We want to go for a last swim today. Don't hold us back, let us go..."

A dagger stabbed my heart over and over, knowing these were the last words I would ever hear from my son again. I knew his hallucinations were now his reality. Still, I forced myself to do everything I could to watch over them. I held on to them so they would not leave the raft and die in the ocean. Was it morbid I wanted them to die in my arms? I no longer cared what my mind was thinking any longer. I would not let them take one last swim. Panic filled my mouth. I tried to swallow the thickness of nothing that was forming inside.

"No, no, no. You are not thinking clearly, my boys. It is unsafe to swim. We need to stay together now." My head throbbed with the words I recently shared. I knew I needed to stay awake. It was so important I watch every breath they took and not allow them to swim or to go overboard. They had no mental clarity. I had more lucidity than them. It was up to me to guide them the way Jackson had done his entire life.

My heart ached for the loss of our lives. The hurt I was feeling was far worse emotionally than physically now.

My babies, I thought of the years I loved them. I refused to allow any doubt to enter my being now. I was a good mother; I loved them more than anything or anyone in life. I protected them like the fierceness of a mother lion. I gave them my heart.

My beautiful Jackson, oh how I adored him. Even though our marriage had been full of sadness because of what I had done, he remained the one constant in my life. We would have died for each other. Now, death was here.

I looked down upon the shells that were my boys. Their breath was almost non-existent. Both had closed their tired eyes again.

My body and mind drifted with the sounds of the ocean. I felt my head nodding unto my chest. We probably had less than an hour to live. I would hold on to them as tight as I could, fighting until the end of my life or theirs. I refused to sleep in our final time together. My eyes were so heavy, though, and my body so tired. I blinked and violently pressed my fingers into my eye sockets to keep from nodding off. I could not allow myself to close my eyes when I knew there was danger in losing them.

I felt my head hit Peter's, and I realized my body was ready to die. I could not control it any longer. A bolt of what felt like electricity surged through my body and into my mind. No, I would not fail them ever again. This would be my last act of living, to protect my sons to the end. I failed them so miserably, but now I would not. I believed if I could keep awake, I could keep them alive. If I could keep them alive, then my life would not have been a waste. My eyes were burning, so I pinched my arm as hard as I could to shock my body into staying awake.

The sun scorched my eyes when I tried to search the distance for one last time. It was too much to investigate any further because of the bright skies. My eyes shut again. It was overwhelming, the sun, the roar of the ocean, I had to sleep. I had to sleep, I told myself, so I could be strong. I inched away from the boys to lie down to slumber. I let go of their little hands and bodies for only a moment. I had not done that for over a day now.

What felt like a few minutes of rest turned into another day. My eyes were open now but crusted over with infection. I could hardly see.

There was something strange that flickered in the distance in the ocean. How could it be? I saw him, I, too, saw Jackson! Why did I not believe them when they both told me they saw him? He was alive! He had found land. There he was, trying to reach us, to bring us back to him. My heartbeat was faster and weaker, but I kept willing myself to keep my eyes on him. He was close enough I could hear him shouting, "Over here! There is life here…"

This *was* a miracle. This was what believers had told me about. Maybe now I would believe it, too. Maybe God doesn't hate me! He was going to save us from our deaths. I promised I would change. Everything would be different now.

The tighter I squeezed my eyes, the more I saw of what looked to be land and people swimming toward us. What was happening? I tried to shout to let them know we were on this raft. I could no longer talk, and I was too weak to lift my hands in the air. There was a smell that invaded my nose, a horrible putrid smell filled the air.

I turned back to where Isaiah and Peter were laying together before I had fallen asleep. I had to know if they saw their Dad and the people, too. I needed them to say it was

Daddy swimming toward us.

When I refocused on them, all that was left was a pile of rags. Their clothes laid on the floor of the raft.

I went wild with despair. I tried to lift a part of my body to look over the side to see if I could see them swimming away, but in my heart, I knew it was useless. They were dead. There was no way they were strong enough to make it to the shore. Their bodies were so emaciated they must have sunk to the ocean floor. There was no strength left in them to go anywhere but down. They had left me. Gone forever. I had let them go. I wanted to ease my body over the side, to join them, but I was too weak to even roll over.

I failed them once again. They were hallucinating so much at the end. I turned my back on them for what I thought was just a minute and they went for the swim they had talked about for the entire time we were lost. How could I have let them go? How could I have been so selfish once again? I was their mother.

Fury rose deep from my soul. *I hate you, God,* I mouthed into the air. How could they call Him good and just when He allowed so much suffering in this world? Why would anyone want to believe in a Deity who killed innocent people? My boys did not deserve to die this way. It should have been me. *Take me, you pitiful God. If You say You are who You are, strike me down now!* There were no thoughts left in my head. I was glad death was here for me. I welcomed it calling out my name.

I let a moan come from my inner being that cracked open what little was left in me. It was the last sound I remember uttering or hearing.

CHAPTER 8

S creams of agony and desperation blasted through the air. My broken body lifted out of the raft by the massive dark hands of a stranger. His black and dirty arms had a hard time holding me still. I wanted to yell at him to leave and not touch me. Instead, panic rose in my throat because I could not speak. My tongue was enlarged and crusted over from dehydration and the many days of floating adrift. My lips split wide open, and infection oozing out. I trembled with fever and fear.

This unknown man kept repeating one word I recognized. These words were the words of a foreigner, a man from a country that was not our own. The language I realized was of the Guyanese. I understood what he said because Jackson created a game many years ago. The premise behind it was for us to memorize ten words from the country where he was volunteering. This one repeated word, echoing into the air, was the one Isaiah and I learned and remembered from many years ago. Peter used to get frustrated when Isaiah and I always won this game. He'd shake his head and say, "I give up, you beat me again." Then he'd wink and say, "But I'll challenge you both to a race any day!"

"Help, help, help," over and over this foreigner repeated. My head so heavy, I could barely move it. My left arm lay stiff and unmovable. My right arm reached toward this man's outstretched hands. It took a great effort to even try to do this.

I was slipping in and out of consciousness. There was one moment when I briefly woke and reflected on how lucky we were to be alive. Now, I will live and every day will be my gift. I will take nothing or no one for granted anymore. Jackson will know we had beaten the odds; we never gave up. I looked back at the raft, hoping I was not hallucinating, and my boys would be in a deep slumber.

My heart was racing. Deep in my heart, I understood these foolish thoughts amounted to nothing more than a lie. Jackson, Lilly and my sons are gone forever. The ocean swallowed them and they would not be found. Their minds had played tricks on them. They no longer understood the difference between fiction and reality.

I wished more than ever to die. I lost everyone who ever loved me. There was no reason for me to stay on this earth one more moment. My purpose for living died the moment they swam away from the raft. I thought I had not slept for very long. It seemed to only be moments from the time they left the raft until this foreigner rescued me. I would never stop blaming myself for sleeping when I recognized how much they had been hallucinating. They should have lived and not me. They did not deserve to die by drowning.

I sensed the chaos closing in on me. This stranger would not stop shouting! Surrounded by a mob of people, I looked at more coming to me from the ocean. The water had disappeared and was, instead, filled with hundreds of people surrounding me. Their hands seemed to want to touch every part of me. I did not want to leave the raft because now it was my only connection to my family.

I tried to speak again, but I only gasped for air, making it impossible for any words to form. *Let me die,* I wanted to say. *Let me drift back into the ocean, never to appear again.* However, his strong hands moved me further away from the life I once perceived as my own. As much as I hated that raft, it saved us for many days. Now I only wanted to die in it.

What did my boys say in their final hours? Did they have a way to hold on to each other? Did they fight the currents or collapse into despair? My imagination stirred wildly, thinking how horrible it must have been for them. I hated myself more than I thought possible.

Their last words to me created more sadness in my heart. How ironic, in all those years, I was posing to be someone else; someone I thought I wanted them to know. In reality, I was that person they always saw. I was only pretending to myself because they had understood the truth long ago. How pathetic I wasted those hours, that turned into days and then years, sensing I needed to protect them from the real me. They realized who I was, yet they loved me still. So many years I missed out on not telling them why I had become the person I now was.

The memories of our final words together filled my heart with sorrow. There was such an incredible ache, I groaned out loud. The stranger's intruding eyes never left mine. I wondered if he could understand what happened to me from my moaning.

Sadness rose in my throat. I turned to these unfamiliar faces and silently screamed. My skin, tight and black, cracked when I opened and shut my mouth. The sobs were so strong that every time I let one out, my body convulsed in pain. Again, I forced myself to stare into this man's face. I met the look of tenderness pouring from this foreigner's dark brown eyes. He held me tight to his chest as if this might soften my cries and take my pain away.

He looked around for a clean place to lay my body. Another man came forward and stripped off his shirt. Two more came. Then three more and they laid their shirts together to form a linen-like sheet on the dark pink sand on the beach. The kind stranger placed me on the pallet. They covered my body so the sting of the sun no longer burned my raw, exposed skin.

Who were these people surrounding me with looks of awe on their faces? I continued to listen to the shrieks of many in the distance. The sounds of wailing and shouting came closer now. My mind did not comprehend why these people surrounded me. Many people cowered over me to look at a defeated, dying woman.

I felt soft hands stroke my face as another lifted my neck to force water into my sore mouth. I closed my lips, knowing I did not want to go on any longer. With my eyes, I tried to plead with them to let me die, to leave me alone, to let me rot on this beach.

The kind faces persisted. I turned away as they forced my mouth open. Even though I desired to die, the taste of the cool, clean water made me greedily open my mouth. I allowed myself to drink what they offered. I drank so much it overflowed onto my chest and spilled onto the soiled ground. The sand had a strange reddish tinge to it but I did not realize at the time what made it this unusual color.

I looked upon a small, frail-looking young woman. She stood out from the people who did not leave my side. She appeared to be moving sideways in a trance-like state. Her torn, pink silk garment trailed behind her. Her hair, a rich dark color, knotted around her temple, hung in tangles below her waist. This vision in pink may have been in her late twenties but it was hard to determine because of the ash covering her face.

She bent down and whispered, "You have come out of the deep ocean to save us. We now have hope. Thank you, our goddess of help. You are what we have been asking the gods to send to us. You will find our missing people. We worship and thank you for answering our pleas," with a thick accent. "Varuni," she repeated over and over and then continued speaking in her native language.

With her last word, I watched as every person dropped to their knees and bowed before me. My fear intensified as I tried to understand what she was saying and why she was saying, "Varuni." I tried to speak to her, to tell her I was no god, that our plane crashed and we drifted for so many days. I wanted her to learn my boys drowned and my husband died in the crash. I had no one left in my life.

She gently placed her head on my heart and continued in her foreign tongue. The aroma of rich lavender exuded through her skin, mingling with the odor of charred flesh. It was then I noticed in horror half of her arm, bandaged in gauze, appeared to dangle by her side. There was a gaping wound where her left elbow used to be, oozing with blood. I looked further and realized her sari was not pink but stained in her own blood.

Her head got heavier as the minutes passed. She never lifted it off me until one man came to her and cradled her lifeless frame in his arms. The woman who had been by her side let out a deep wail like the raw sound of a wounded animal. I understood from her cry she must be the mother of this magnificent dead woman.

The continuous roar of the people became unbearable. What were they doing and what did they want from me? I could only move my head a few inches to look beyond the mob of people surrounding me. Why were they covered with blood? What was that loud noise and screaming that came from beyond this place where I lay?

Suddenly, I was being carried away again. It felt more like I was floating in the air, and I was. Each person held out their arms and passed me along to the next person in line. There was so much blood on their arms, but I had no strength to escape their firm clutches.

The many hours of my moving further down the line abruptly came to a halt. They carried me into a small demolished home and laid me upon a bed. I looked around to consider how I might escape from these people and this place, but there were too many of them crowded into this tiny space. There were no clues as to what they wanted of me or what they would do once they realized I was not a god.

The men disappeared, leaving me surrounded by the faces of many exotic-looking ladies. In each of their eyes, I perceived such sadness and shock, dimming their real beauty. I tried to move from the bed but many gentle hands reached and grabbed ahold of my arms and legs.

One striking lady, who looked my age, took my hand. With a strange but lulling voice, she sang with a sense of despair. Her tears dropped from her eyes and stung the open sores on my face. Something fluttered in my womb and I recognized she, too, had lost a son or daughter. I wanted to hold on to her, but other women pushed her aside so they, too, could touch my shattered frame. This mother had no choice but to let go, but I never let my eyes leave hers. She stood aside and her hysteria could no longer be contained. She fell to the floor and cried out again, "Varuni!" Men came to her and carried her out into the daylight. In this short interchange between us, it felt I had lost someone I had known my entire life. How is the universal grief of losing a child known by no words? Her eyes will haunt me for the rest of my life as I realized mine will for her.

I had no more time to consider the grief of that childless woman. The others now removing my tattered rags, the smell of sweet primrose oil poured into the air and onto my skin. Everyone took turns washing me and saying the same words over and over. Their kind touch was too much for my heart to bear. I closed my eyes and fell into a deep and troubled sleep.

When I finally awoke, there was no light. The darkness was

even deeper than we had experienced on the raft. I shuttered to remember I was alive, but my sons had floated away into darkness, never to be recovered. I had no sight, but my hearing was heightened. It was strange; the stillness emerging from the earth. However, there also arose an unbearable and constant wailing that seemed to rise from the depths of this land.

The people of Guyana had left me alone in the blackness to wallow in my grief. I needed to leave this bed, to escape. I had nowhere to go, but wanted to wander back into the ocean to join my sons.

Now able to adjust my arms and legs, I attempted to climb out of the bed, but in my weakness I collapsed to the floor.

Upon hearing the thud, a man, hidden by the night and sleeping in the chair next to my bed, called out in the darkness, "Do not move, little one. I take you back to slumber for more nights."

There was no resisting the stranger's arms around my waist. I was too weak right now to leave and so I allowed him to carry me to the comfort of the feather bed.

I gulped deeply and attempted to speak to him. The pain was unbearable so instead I watched as he reached over to the nightstand which held a tattered Bible. He poured warm, dingy water into a cup and he held my head back to receive it.

I slept again; restless with dread, unable to turn without a stabbing pain.

When I woke, I tried desperately to form words. "Who are you? Where am I? I want to go home," I cried out in distress, knowing deep in my heart, this wasn't possible. I waited a few moments before asking again, "Where am I? Who are you people?"

I looked at the whites in his eyes. The kindness shone from his face and I finally acknowledged these people meant me no harm. He leaned as close as possible to my ear to drown out the screaming of the outside world. "My name is Latchman. I tell you what I am. I live here always." His words exuded warmth and comfort, yet sent a chill down my spine. "We had a good and prosperous life. I provide well for my wife and daughter and my wife's family. We have abundance in this land. Two days ago, our families together, eating, working, laughing. Babies born, old people dying..." His voice trailed off to a whisper. He shook his head as if to clean every wrong thought from his memory.

"Our people, I have lost every people everywhere. They disappear from everyone they loved. The sound you pick up now, it started when the planes fell from the skies and the cars smash into each other. Everything became confused. No electricity, nothing but the odor of death and decay. There was nowhere to hide. My wife and daughter sit next to me at one minute. We eat. I rest on chair; I close my eyes for one second, I promise you, I no lie. One second and then I look to them and they disappear...gone forever.

"Their clothes, just their clothes left behind. I figure out this must be a trick; my neighbor is making them disappear and they will be here soon. I always felt him to have laughs on me. He made it every day to come over and show me new magic he read in his book. I call to him; I try to use my phone and nothing there. I walk to his door and yell and yell for him to make them come back. I look in the window and he is sitting and will not move. Next to him is a pile of what I think his wife's dress. Screaming and wailing, louder and louder. I learn so many people are not here, are somewhere, but far away. People walking and even crawling on the streets, like wild animals they are. No one understands what did this, how it be so.

"Many of us come together that day. We hug and cry and we look to see who's here and who gone. No one understands who took so many. My people; they turned to our gods for an answer. We bow to our gods and seek them to tell us answers.

Everyone stands in that spot on the sand and then, after kneeling, we rise. Then we look into the sea. You came to us, a white god, that rose from the ocean. Like you fall from the sky. We see you are the answer to what we must learn. So, we look to you to guide us to our people, to find our children, our family, our friends. You can bring us to them. We felt that you came to lead us to our families. None of us will grieve more. We will bow to you and say you have heard our cries."

I felt his pain deep inside me. They thought, without a doubt, I could make their families reappear. It made me understand that I was so much like them now. How I wished I could believe in someone to bring my children, my husband and my life back.

I felt even more helpless than I did on the raft. How would I ever be able to explain to them I could not even save my own children from drowning? Wasn't it just today I was holding my sweet sons in my arms? Now I've realized it was at least several days ago they left me. I missed them more than I could ever imagine. I thought the ache I had felt after losing Catherine and Grace was the worst pain I might ever endure. No, this searing agony burned inside my mind and my heart. It robbed me of even the good memories because I had such guilt from being alive.

Blackness filled my mind at the fate of my husband and sons. I did not want to remember my life any longer. There was nothing in my heart but pain. I died again, but this time I felt it was for the last time.

Jackson was dead. I had turned away from him instead of reaching out to save him, as he had tried to save me. The boys, too, were gone forever. I let them slip away into nothingness. I felt complete blackness in my soul. I had only myself to blame for their deaths. I allowed, once again, to let the people I treasure the most in my life to die.

He shushed me. "You need rest before you tell where my wife and daughter go."

He informed me I had been asleep for many days. A doctor had visited me every morning since they brought me here. The healer said he had a vision and it showed him the god in this bed needed to gain strength for the journey to look for everyone. They had no place to go and would wait here for me to be strong. Once I was okay to move, I needed to show him and everyone from his city where their families went.

He said, "Everyone is waiting to follow you. No one will harm you, never to fear. We will walk to wherever we need to go. We want to be with our loved humans."

As much as I wanted him to go away, there was something inside of me that needed him to speak. "Tell me again. I won't sleep until you tell me, again, what happened to your people."

With even more sadness in his voice, he wearily told me more of his story.

He looked away from me and his eyes focused on an old, tattered Bible. Bitterness replaced the sadness in his voice. His soft words grew louder and darker.

Pointing an accusatory finger at the Bible, he cried, "I tell you now. It is this book that make my wife and daughter not like before. They find it two years ago, and they change. They looked the same, but there was new in their eyes. My wife telling me I need to read it with her. She wish I go to a building they call church in the next town. They leave for there every Sunday and left me sitting alone in my chair.

"How she be not the same? How she not accepts what we know? She take my daughter with her to that place! Every time she came from there, she was little different. Her eyes even looking unlike before. She no longer wore her custom dress. My friends, they laugh at me and say, 'She is no longer your wife.' They threaten me to remove her from our home. I love her and daughter and would never try to hurt them. She belong with me and she was still the woman my parents arrange me to marry. The more time went on she no longer allow our gods in our house. Never again she kneel to my gods and worship them. She took every single statue and place in a box outside my home. I should not let her do this to me. She make me a fool in front of my people. I not fight her because I love her and daughter more than any god I worshiped. I thought in my heart they love me. My friends, they tell everyone I am not a man any longer. I get bitter and angry.

"One day, I hear their prayers to the man they called Jesus.

They pray for my soul and for my heart to soften. They now scare me. What are they going to do? Why they want my heart to melt? I yell at them and told them I would not let them to go away from me no more. My wife plead with me and try to tell me their God and His boy was the only way to get to heaven. I have not know of this place they call heaven. I no need for none of it. I know everything lives has soul, from Brahman. We teached that all us souls live on after death, and everything be reborn. Reincarnation is all we have. How I want to have beliefs for a man they say was died? Even worse, they pretend he come back alive again? They tell he no reincarnate but come back as Himself? Hinduism is what we have. My parents, brothers and sisters, Hindus. That is all we ever got teached and all we have to know.

"I no listen to them. I make my head up; they now want me hurt. I shake my fist in wife face. I spit mad at her. So mad. My wife, no angry back. She only say she love me. And she only have eye that look nice. No mean in her. I sad to hurt her. I tell you I love her and my baby girl too much to be so bad. I still tell I will not see them leave my home.

"But, oh, I remember one of their last days they here. My sweet little one place her tiny little hand in mine, begged me to let her go on Sunday. She cry and say for me to come with them. My wife kneel before me and had such pain and loved mixed in together. She told me she love me but she choose this God over me! She says she take my daughter away if I did not let them to go to place she say is her new home! My heart feels smashed at her words. I look at my lovely daughter, I never resist her big almond color eyes. She smiles at me and says, 'Daddy, we need you with us. We are a family. We want you to be saved, too.'

"I am lost my little love, is that right?

"She nodded at me and said, 'Yes, Daddy, you are.'

"Something I feel in my heart, right at that time. I no tell anyone, but I think my heart getting warm. I hold her close and I promise to her and my wife. I say right then me to go with them to that place they said make them alive for their first time in this world. I am so tired of seeing your sadness when I talk so hard to you. I say to them I, too, need for a happiness and peace they carry.

"But now they vanish and I tried to go to the place in that town, not there. Destroyed by my people who tear it apart, stone by stone, looking for the ones they love. It is gone with them."

When Latchman looked me in the eyes again, his words chilled me. "It was their God took them. That loving God they say took my love from me. Now, we must find them because He has hidden them. How can He be love if He bring this pain in suffering? How did He allow someone to take away them? Everything gone except darkness and fear. I will find them and make them never leave me again. I will allow no one to take them from me," he cried.

He stared off into the darkness, his sadness seeping through the walls of this home. "I tell you," he said, "how terrible for my wife sister. She was to have baby. Her belly was round and now nothing left of her. Gone. He took the baby, too. I am sure. Her man walks around crazed faced. I cannot look at him, he blames me, my wife gave her book that caused us this badness. How terrible for her!"

"Wait, wait, wait," I murmured to him. "What you said, how terrible for a pregnant woman..." I could no longer lay in the bed. With all my strength, I sat up and I looked at this tired man and told him, "I know!" I understood and knew where his family had gone and who had taken them forever. "You are right regarding most of the details of their disappearance. God had taken them away." But it was not a tragedy. His family and those that vanished were safe now. They're in a place that holds no more pain or sorrow.

I shook my head with this incredulous knowledge. With not one doubt in my mind, I realized where Peter and Isaiah were at this very moment. My loves did not go for one last swim as I had thought! They, too, were lifted into the air, along with every believer on this earth. The rapture had spirited them to heaven. My family was in paradise today. Reunited with Jackson, our families and friends, together for eternity!

I was still too weak to move. He must come closer so I could tell him the truth of what happened to his family and the rest of the world. I recognized what I needed to do. I asked him to lift me out of the bed and onto the damp dark floor. The many thoughts I had buried in my heart for years cracked it wide apart.

God had spared me for this moment, to bring me to this point in my life. He showed mercy on me when the plane crashed, and on the raft when I should have died. He loved me enough to wait for me to admit I was nothing without Him; that I needed a Savior. After years of doubt, anger, and mistrust, I had to do what I had never allowed myself to do before.

I placed my hand on God's Word and knelt on the floor. I asked God to forgive me for the years I had turned my back on Him. With no fear of what Latchman expected of me, I brought my sins to Jesus. I poured my heart out to Him. I cried tears of sorrow and regret. Tears of love and joy. I recognized what was happening; I remembered Jackson telling me stories of people being born again.

Now I was the one experiencing the first of many miracles to come. Peace poured into my heart and overflowed inside me. I looked around the room and noticed colors like I had never seen before; everything was brighter. Nothing was the same. My heart, which had carried the burden of guilt and shame, healed instantaneously. Oh, this was what my family had known for so many years! The peace...the peace that surpasses all understanding caused me to mouth again and again, "Amazing grace how sweet the sound..."

I looked over at this man who stood before me. He, too, was a helpless, broken person who needed a Savior. I longed for him to understand what I had received. I wanted everyone to share in this uncontainable joy. I stood, and he looked at me with wide disbelief.

"You are up; you walk?"

"Yes," I said, "I can walk. I am healed!"

He shook his head. "Show yourself! You are a god; you have healed yourself!" He did not understand what happened. He continued to beg and plead with me to help him find his family.

I opened the Bible and repeated the same message I had read many times before.

Jackson loved preaching on the book of Revelation. He always said it was the most misunderstood book in the Bible. This time, though, as I read it, it was different. The words had meaning. Rather than hearing it with my ears, I spoke it with my heart. It was as if the words became alive and I needed to share them with Latchman.

Latchman looked at me with confused eyes. He cried out loud, "There something has happened to you. I look at it; I can see it. I fear of this book. I felt it now will take you away with my family and you will not bring them back."

This poor man wanted nothing more than to find his family. I understood this pain and because of this, a sudden, strong bond developed between us. He felt like family. I squeezed his hand and cried for his loss. His despair came from the pits of his soul. I told him, "There is a way, a way you will be with your beloved wife and daughter someday." He looked at me with such disbelief I had to take his hand again and tell him the truth. I had to make him understand the value of the gift anyone who called upon the Lord received.

I read and reread from the Word until my throat was raw. I looked at him and realized he was beginning to supernaturally understood what was in the Bible.

After what seemed like hours, he whispered into my ear, "I am ready to get it now. I am ready to learn what you tell me. Will this hurt me a lot?"

I spoke deliberately to him so he might understand me.

"You might go through unbearable pain for what you've lost, but you will welcome an incredible joy for what you will receive."

"Months go by and I did not want to listen. If I had, now I would not be here alone." He looked at me. "But what wrong with you? Why are you left behind with me and so many of my people?"

I told him everything regarding my family, and the secrets I had hidden away for many years. I had no shame when I exposed myself to him. I learned God had forgiven me now for the wrongs I had committed in my lifetime. The demons gone, forever cast out of my mind and soul.

"I am scared. What if He no want me? What if I am too dirt?"

"Salvation is a gift from God. We do nothing to deserve this."

He kept shaking his head. "I awful; I not a good man."

"I understand; I had felt that way, too, for many years."

"Okay, maybe, if you can do it, I can, too. I am tired of alone. I want to look at my wife and daughter. I want to go where they have gone." Latchman knelt beside me and, with my hand on his shoulder, he asked God to come into his heart. He then stood, his mouth wide open, and wiped away the tears, exposing his radiant smile. I recognized he was now a changed man. This man, who was once an unknown person to me, hugged me. When he released me, I felt this gentle and sweet man would no longer be a stranger.

After reading more of the Bible, the words began to get jumbled and dark. I laid this Book of Truth on the stand and lay upon the bed. As I lay there thanking Him for His mercy, I heard a voice in my heart that quietly said, *Bittersweet.* Every emotion I kept locked in my heart washed over me and forced me into a deep slumber. For the first time in many years, I did not fight it. I realized I had nothing to fear any longer. When I closed my eyes, what started out as a nightmare turned into a lovely dream.

As I prepared the meal in the sunny kitchen surrounded by the aroma of lilacs drifting through the open window, I peer in the mirror in front of me. I was filled with darkness, and a stranger on this earth. There was nowhere to hide, secrets exposed for everyone to examine. My family left without me, gone to a place they called paradise. Why was I not allowed to follow them? I was here, waiting to receive it, too. I would wait here forever, alone, with no joy or laughter to fill my heart. I rejected the truth by turning from it. I assumed I knew what it was like to be a good person, to get to heaven because I did the right things for most of my life. However, I failed and now I stood with no mask, revealing the real me. The guilt I clung to for my life became my idol. It became my identity. No matter how many times I tried to drown out the voices in my head, they only got stronger as I became weaker.

As I reminisced on my husband, sons, and parents, I peered at my reflection in the mirror and wondered, Did you always recognize the truth my dear family? Did you always notice I rejected Jesus because I felt I was too filthy with sin? The irony was, my pride kept me from the One who cleansed and made us whole. I never wanted to be an evil girl. I have made Jesus weep because I refused to accept His love and grace. My family accepted the truth from the moment they received it. If they had any doubts, they never told me. They loved the Lord, and they each gave Him their hearts. Why, oh why, did I not listen to them and His pleas of love?

I looked out the window upon a remarkable cocoon hanging on the tree. In the blink of an eye, a butterfly emerges. God laid it upon my heart. I looked and found it was me! I, too, was transformed. So many years I was afraid to escape the self-imposed prison of pride and doubt.

"Mom!"

"Mommy!"

Their cries filled my ears and cloaked my heart in warmth.

"It's you."

"You are here."

I looked away from the butterfly spinning in the air. They appeared around the table. Their bodies were whole again and nothing but joy appeared on their faces.

"We will wait for you. When it's your time, Daddy will meet you, too!"

Awakening from my dream, I realized today would be another day I would dwell on them, but now, instead of the constant aching of sadness, I had hope and knowledge I would be with each of them again. God had used the years I wasted to get me to this place I now called home.

Over six years had passed since the day I lost my old life, but God gave me a new one. I am married to the stranger who rescued me from the sea. Our decision to join together at first was not an easy one. We both grieved separately until we understood we had a purpose in becoming man and wife. I heard the voices of condemnation begin again, after we told Latchman's people of our intentions. However, the voice of God was stronger and louder. I no longer believed a lie told from the enemy of my soul.

I glanced at my pretty daughter. We named her Amarisa, because in Hebrew it means Given by God. She was now five years old and was our miracle. No doctor's explanations given on how I conceived after being barren for years. We trusted God gave her to us as a sign of His love.

Amarisa sang faintly to her new puppy, telling her she must learn to be a good girl and grow up to be like Lilly. I smiled at her childlike innocence. I spoke to her often of her beautiful brothers in heaven. Although she never met them, she said she knew they watch over her. She saw them in her dreams, too. I did not question this and knew she spoke the truth. There were many details I never told her. Amarisa gave me vivid descriptions of their appearances in her dreams. She had so much of them inside her. I tenderly watched my daughter as her song grew into a whisper. Something made her smile and look up to the sky. Her musical laughter filled the air and the empty place that sometimes filled my heart.

Latchman and I have started a journey to save all whom are lost. The tribulation has brought much violence and despair to many. He reminded me today we must go. We must leave the comforts of our home and try to reach people who needed to receive His word. We had work to do in this city. Everything laid in ruins so many years ago. However, with love it would grow strong again. Never would it be as rich as it once was, but we learned the treasures we had now were what we always needed. We were here to bring others to the church. Latchman and I both admitted our losses had brought us here to these people. I experienced the truth for many years, but fear and pride made me accept a lie. We were sure, without a doubt, we would live with our families and Jesus and His Father someday.

"Come now, we have work to do." He reminded me every day I was strong now and never had to look back on my shame. "Your wings are no longer broken, and you can fly like soaring eagles. You must bring the truth of God's love and mercy and healing to everyone."

As I stood, I looked incredulously at the fullness of my body. A new life was again growing inside of me. We were blessed to have another miracle in our lives. The ultrasound showed us a healthy and beautiful boy would enter our world. My physical wounds healed, but the scars would linger forever. I was okay with that. It took that pain and loss to open my eyes. To understand no sin, no poor choice in this life would ever keep us from the love of the only one who could heal us and make us new.

There were some rare days when I dwelled on the pain of losing Jackson, Peter, Isaiah, and even Lilly. I sometimes became so overwhelmed I couldn't bear the pain from what I lost. The intensity would hit me so hard I could only fall to the floor and plead with God to remove the sorrow. However, His words reminded me He had overcome the pain and suffering in this broken world. He, too, endured the loss of His son.

I could and would go on knowing one day I would be with our Father and my family again. I go on because there was still so much of His work to do in this world.

Want to know how the real story ends? Read a Bible. I promise you will find all the answers.

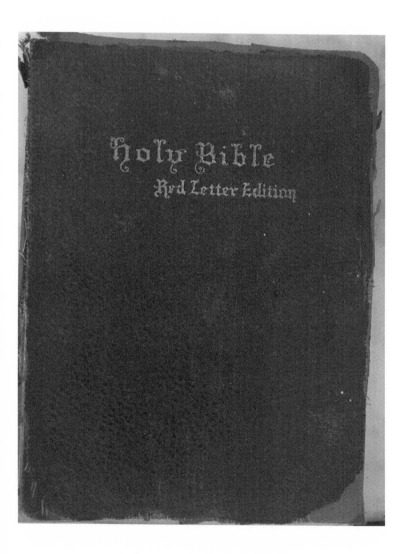

About the Author

A native of Saratoga, New York, Debra Geiman Colletti now calls Myrtle Beach, South Carolina, her home, where she resides with Michael, her supportive husband, and their three dogs: Ciara, a Boston Terrier/Pit Bull, and two Pugs: Max and Rosa.

When she's not writing, she travels back to New York to visit her two sons, their spouses, and two beautiful grandbabies. When not in New York, she visits her Florida family.

Author's Note

Approximately five years ago, I told my son, Nicholas, about a dream I had the night before. His first response was, "Wow, you ought to write a book about it." If it weren't for his encouragement then and throughout this process, I would not have had the courage to continue.

Several of my friends and family who have read this book ask me if it is based upon my life. This is a work of fiction, although the story drew upon my fundamental belief of Jesus's love. The characters are fictional. Are there some similarities? Of course. I do not think any writer can develop individuals without allowing themselves and loved ones to show up.

I am including several different resources for some of the topics that have been touched upon in this book. Please know you are not alone. Seek help; I promise someone is always willing to guide you.

Addiction and Mental Health
www.samhsa.gov

Adoption
http://www.adoption.com/
http://www.apreciousgiftarc.com/

Aftermath of Abortion
https://www.rachelsvineyard.org

Fostering
https://www.davethomasfoundation.org/

Mental Health
www.nami.org

Pro-Life
www.personhood.org

Sudden Infant Death Syndrome
Www.sids.org

Suicide Prevention
http://www.afsp.org

Made in the USA
Middletown, DE
12 April 2021